Another Prairie Grave...

"I think we can git started now, Massa John."

Stone reached into his boot and pulled out his Apache knife.

Stone and Ephraim looked at each other, blades shining. Ephraim saw the symbol of everything he hated in the world... and nothing else in the world mattered now. They looked for an opening, a nuance, the telltale sign that betrayed vulnerability. because you only make one mistake in a knife fight: your first...

This book also contains a preview of Nelson Nye's exciting new western novel, *The Last Chance Kid.*

Also in the SEARCHER series by Josh Edwards

SEARCHER
LYNCH LAW
TIN BADGE
WARPATH
HELLFIRE
DEVIL'S BRAND

SEARCHER
STAMPEDE

Josh Edwards

DIAMOND BOOKS, NEW YORK

STAMPEDE

A Diamond Book / published by arrangement
with the author

PRINTING HISTORY
Diamond edition / February 1992

All rights reserved.
Copyright © 1992 by Charter Communications, Inc.
Material excerpted from *The Last Chance Kid* by Nelson Nye
copyright © 1992 by Nelson Nye.
This book may not be reproduced in whole or in part,
by mimeograph or any other means, without permission.
For information address: The Berkley Publishing Group,
200 Madison Avenue, New York, New York 10016.

ISBN: 1-55773-664-2

Diamond Books are published by The Berkley Publishing Group,
200 Madison Avenue, New York, New York 10016.
The name "DIAMOND" and its logo are trademarks
belonging to Charter Communications, Inc.

PRINTED IN THE UNITED STATES OF AMERICA

10 9 8 7 6 5 4 3 2 1

1

THE COWBOYS FROM the Triangle Spur sat around the campfire, eating steak and beans. It was night, a chill was on the prairie, and the indigo sky was splattered with stars. The men were exhausted, clothes torn, fingernails caked with dirt. On the trail nearly a week, it was a constant struggle to keep the longhorns shaped, bunched, and pointed toward Abilene.

Near the flames, John Stone leaned against his saddle, his old Confederate cavalry hat on the back of his head. His clothes were covered with dust, and it permeated his dark blond hair and beard. This was his first cattle drive, and he rode the drag.

The other men were as bedraggled and beat as he. They were the usual assortment of misfits, vagabonds, adventurers, and desperadoes, firelight flicking on their bearded faces, because nobody had the time, energy, or inclination to shave. Some had driven longhorns to Abilene before, while others like Stone were making their first trip. They knew hardship lay ahead, and other cowboys had died violently on the trail, ending up in lonely graves on the tractless wastes, but so far the drive had been without incident.

Nearby, on a grassy Texas plain, the herd was like a great sullen being, spread over a few hundred acres. It could trample the cowboys to smithereens, but so far grudgingly advanced ten miles a day toward the slaughterhouses of the East.

There was no hint of the blood and guts of that showdown now. The night was still, mountains and buttes glowing in the light of the full moon. A log fell in the fire, showering sparks into the sky.

Stone finished his last scoop of beans and lay his tin plate on the ground. Broad-shouldered, six feet four, he wore two Colts in crisscrossed gunbelts, with the holsters tied to his legs gunfighter style. He poked a twig into the fire, it caught flame, and he lit the cigarette.

He was ready to turn in, and felt like a productive citizen for a change. He hadn't touched whiskey since hitting the trail, and the exercise was toughening him. For the past three months he'd been drunk nearly all the time, but now was on his way back to strength and health.

Stone's dream was to straighten out his life and become a rancher with his own herd, family—everything a decent man would want. He'd joined the Triangle Spur to learn the cattle business, starting at the bottom. That was the plan, but he had one major problem.

Shadows danced on the canvas walls of the chuck wagon, where Ephraim, the Negro cook, sat on the wagon tongue, eating his meal. Ephraim looked up, and his eyes met Stone's.

Deep visceral malevolence passed between them. By a freak quirk of circumstance, Ephraim had been one of John Stone's father's slaves before the war, and hated Stone with fierce passion. Once, in a dark alley in San Antone, they'd clashed fiercely, bloodying each other considerably, but with no clear-cut winner—the fight had been interrupted by townspeople. Now they were looking for the opportunity to be alone somewhere, and finish the job.

Ephraim was only one of Stone's problems. He looked to the right of the chuck wagon, and saw the buckboard and tent of Cassandra Whiteside, the boss lady, who unfortunately bore a strong resemblance to Marie, Stone's former fiancée.

Stone had been searching for Marie since the end of the war. Like a tramp he'd made his way across the frontier, showing her picture in every saloon, church, and pool hall, encountering one disappointment after another. He thought he'd struck paydirt near Tucson a few months ago, when a rancher told him he'd seen the lady in San Antone, but when Stone finally reached San Antone, he found Cassandra Whiteside instead. It had been a major disappointment, the last in a long line.

Cassandra offered him a job with the Triangle Spur, and he decided to give up his search for Marie. Five years of futility across the length and breadth of the frontier had turned him into a drunkard and a bumbling fool. Now he wanted to learn the cattle business and find someone else to marry.

But first there was Ephraim. One of these days they'd go off behind a hill, or into the cottonwoods, and battle it out with knives, fists, guns, it didn't matter. There wasn't enough room in the world for both of them.

No one else knew of their vendetta. If they clashed in front of the others, Ephraim would be hung from the nearest tree for daring to fight a white man. Neither wanted anybody to stop them once they started beating on each other, so they bided their time, and in a few days, when things settled down, they'd get it on.

They glowered at each other over the crackling flames. *I'll cut your heart out and feed it to the coyotes,* Ephraim's eyes seemed to be saying. *I'll kick your ass,* Stone replied.

Cassandra Whiteside sat on the cot inside her tent, illuminated by an ornate brass coal-oil lamp hanging from the ridgepole. She was twenty-three years old, bone-tired, and hadn't had a bath since San Antone. Her golden hair was pulled to a bun behind her head, and she worried about her future.

She had three thousand head of mixed longhorns, and was in debt to her eyeballs. Her former husband had kept a chorus girl on the side, made bad investments, stole most of her inheritance, and tried to murder her, but now he was dead, she was free from his wicked power, in a desperate struggle to repair her financial stability. The ramrod told her the drive might last two or three months, depending on trail conditions, the mood of the Indians, the proliferation of rustlers, and so on. She was afraid creditors might show up any moment, demanding cattle as payment.

The longhorns were worth eight dollars a head in Texas, but twenty-two in Abilene. If she could make it all the way to that great cattle mecca, she'd be out of debt, with enough capital for a new venture, but if anything went wrong she could end up a prostitute in the Last Chance Saloon. The frontier was hell on horses and women, and Cassandra had been learning the hard way. She'd been well off before the war, with servants and party dresses, but now had to think and plan like a man.

The problem was she didn't know cattle, and had to rely on her ramrod, Duke Truscott, an irascible old cowpoke with a hide like an armadillo, who treated her like an idiot. The cowboys laughed behind her back and made fun of her. They cast suggestive glances in her direction. She was alone with fourteen men in the middle of nowhere, and sometimes worried they'd rip off her shirt and jeans.

She felt half aroused and half terrified. They were a rough assortment of hard-drinking American cowboys and Mexican vaqueros, some natural gentlemen, others brutes like Braswell, the *segundo*. Ahead were several hundred miles of obstacles and serious danger, but the worst part was loneliness.

Prior to leaving the ranch, she'd become somewhat friendly with John Stone, but there was no time for chitchat on the trail. He worked the herd, while she rode the buckboard. At night he stayed with the cowboys around the campfire, avoiding her. He'd been acting peculiarly since the first moment they'd met at the Triangle Spur Ranch.

She knew what his problem was: he'd told her everything about Marie. But telling hadn't been enough, he was spooked by her. As for her, she needed somebody to talk with. She couldn't make it all the way to Abilene without human contact.

She finished her meal, and went outside to wash her tin plate. A bucket of water sat on the ground near a buckboard wheel, and she dipped the plate in. She heard approaching hoofbeats, and out of the night rode Ray Slipchuck, the former stagecoach driver, atop his lineback dun, returning from the herd. A wiry man in his sixties, with numerous missing teeth, he touched a finger to the brim of his battered hat as he approached.

"How's the herd, Mr. Slipchuck?" she asked.

"I'd say they was 'bout a-ready fer a stampede, ma'am."

She forced her voice toward calm. "I think you'd better relay that information to Mr. Truscott right away."

Slipchuck leaned on his saddle horn and grinned. "He knows all about it, ma'am. By the way, I seen a little stream back there. If'n you wanted to take a bath, I'd be happy to watch out fer you, case there's Comanche around."

If he guarded her, who'd guard him? "No thank you, Mr. Slipchuck. I'm too tired to go anywhere right now. Do you think you could ask Mr. Stone to come to my tent, please?"

Slipchuck rode toward the campfire, and Cassandra returned to her tent, already having second thoughts about asking Stone to visit her. The words had left her mouth before she knew what happened, but loneliness forced the issue.

She sat on her cot and fidgeted nervously. A bath would be nice, but she was afraid to take off her clothes in the open, with the men around, and stand naked before them in the moonlight.

But her main problem was what to do if creditors showed up. There'd probably be gunplay, because her men were hotheaded—they'd fought for her back at the ranch. They were good men deep down, sometimes so deep you couldn't see it, but unfortunately they were also low-class drunkards and louts, and she wouldn't put anything past them.

She heard approaching footsteps, and then Stone said, "Cassandra?"

"Who else did you think was in this tent?" she asked. "Of course it's me."

He entered the tent and saw her sitting on the cot, her long shapely legs crossed, and he thought it amazing that she looked so much like Marie. They were almost twins, and he wanted to kiss her, but she was the wrong person. He waited for her to tell him what to do, because she was boss lady, and he rode the drag.

"Have a seat, John," she said.

He dropped onto a camp chair. "Mind if I smoke?"

"That's your business, but do you think we could have a conversation? I'm so bored I could scream."

"Aren't you tired?"

"Do you think the buckboard runs by itself? Of course I'm tired, but I need someone to speak with for a few minutes, some intellectual stimulation and good Christian fellowship. That won't be such a chore, will it?"

Stone wanted not only to talk with her, but spend the night with her as well, and at the same time felt the mad urge to run out of the tent, because she reminded him of Marie. "If I spend time with you, the men'll get suspicious. They'll think I'm spying on them and reporting to you, and pretty soon one'll put a bullet in my back. I enjoy your company very much, Cassandra, but if you want to talk with somebody, you should talk to Truscott."

"Truscott hates me. He thinks I don't know anything, and I certainly don't know much about cattle, but by God I'll learn."

"He's scared to death of you, because the only women he ever sees are in whorehouses. If you want to talk, why don't you come to the campfire? We're just sitting around, and you might as well join us. It's going to be a long trip."

"Those cowboys don't want me around."

"You've got it all wrong. They're crazy about you."

She hugged her arms. "I'm afraid of them sometimes."

"They'd never do anything to you, except for the *segundo*. Don't ever be alone with the *segundo*."

"The man's obviously a rapist and murderer," she said with a grim smile. "I should've fired him long ago."

"He's the worst we've got, no doubt about that. But the others aren't so bad, and some're quite interesting. C'mon—it's time to get friendlier with your cowboys."

He grabbed her arm and pulled her out of the tent, she digging the heels of her cowboys boots into the ground, trying to break loose from his grip, but he was too strong, and moved her easily into the night. The cowboys at the fire turned to look at them, and she realized she'd better stop struggling. He turned her loose, she smoothed her hair and made sure her shirt was buttoned.

She walked beside Stone to the fire, and all the cowboys examined her with the eyes of whorehouse connoisseurs. A few licked their lips absentmindedly, wild-eyed range riders with scraggly beards and dirty clothes, who made way as she and Stone approached the fire.

Stone cleared his throat. "Mrs. Whiteside thought she'd like to sit with you boys for a while."

The cowboys appeared uneasy, and nobody said anything. Cassandra sat on the ground, but a wooden crate appeared out of the night, in the hands of Luke Duvall, who was wanted for murder in Georgia and who wore a rope scar around his neck.

"Ma'am," he muttered nervously.

"Thank you," she replied.

Stone dropped to the ground beside her. A fidgety silence pervaded the campfire. She assumed they'd been talking, but now had stopped, disturbed by her presence.

"Just go on with what you were doing," she said. "Don't let me interrupt you."

The silence wouldn't go away. Somebody threw a log on the fire, and orange diamonds burst into the air. Cassandra realized she was intruding into their lives. She shouldn't've let John Stone talk her into coming here.

She glanced surreptitiously at the cowboys, and they were all staring into the fire, paying no attention to her. They were in the daze of exhaustion, after fighting the herd all day, and soon would curl up on the ground in their blankets, beneath the open sky.

She decided to relax with them, and didn't feel lonely anymore. Letting her mind wander, the fire flickered and flashed, and deep in the white-hot embers she perceived the face of her ex-husband, Gideon Whiteside. He'd been evil incarnate, yet she'd loved and trusted him, given him everything. He'd seemed a gentleman, and her cowboys uneducated ruffians, yet he'd tried to kill her, and they saved her.

She heard cattle lowing in the distance, and could feel their colossal primordial potential for destruction. She turned to Truscott and said, "Mr. Slipchuck told me he thought the herd might stampede tonight. Do you think we should take precautions?"

Truscott was in his mid-forties, with deep-lined weather-beaten features and a droopy graying mustache. "Like what?"

"Ah . . . I don't know. Surely there must be something you can do."

"Such as?"

"If they stampede, how'll you stop them?"

"If they stampede, they cain't be stopped. All we can do is try to mill 'em till they run theirselves out."

Truscott threw his cigarette butt into the fire. Cassandra felt two eyes burning into her, and turned to the *segundo* staring at her. He had close-spaced eyes, and shot her a lewd wink, turning up one corner of his blubbery lips. She wondered what sheriff was looking for him.

The *segundo*'s hand caressed the head of his mongrel dog, a mangy, bony cur with a filthy white and black coat and one black eye. The *segundo* and his dog were inseparable, and slept together every night.

She turned away, and this time her eyes fell on Don Emilio Maldonado, the Mexican rancher who'd joined the drive the day before it left, along with his vaqueros. They'd had a scrape with the law in the brush country near the Nueces, and a bloody bandage was visible on his forehead beneath his wide sombrero. Most of his men were shot up too, but Mexican vaqueros were the best cowboys in the world, and Cassandra would hire the Devil if he could help her get the herd to Abilene.

Don Emilio gazed at her unflinchingly, and the expression in his eyes said he wanted her. Cassandra turned away, and this time her eyes fell on lean Calvin Blakemore, who had a thick black beard and wore an old Yankee forage cap; he'd been a sergeant in the Yankee army, and now was learning the cowboy trade. He too had depravity in his eyes, and an expression that left no doubts about his dishonorable intentions, but unlike the *segundo*, he tried to be a gentleman.

She shifted her focus to Ephraim the cook, and he too was looking at her, but showed not the faintest trace of interest, because he knew the white cowboys would hang him if he did.

She slapped a bug on her arm, and her eyes fell on John Stone's profile. His hat was low over his eyes, flames danced on his face, and a cigarette dangled out the corner of his mouth. He'd commanded a troop of Confederate cavalry in the bloodiest battles the world had ever seen, but now had become moody, withdrawn, and a drunk like the rest of them.

Truscott cleared his throat, and when his voice came, it sounded as though it were traveling over five miles of bad road. "I'm turnin' in," he said. "Breakfast at four-thirty, trail at five."

The men stood, burped, and farted. John Stone moved sluggishly toward his blanket, and Cassandra realized she'd have to walk back to her tent alone. She pulled her shawl around her shoulders and turned from the fire.

She washed her face and hands in the basin, then entered her tent. It was pitch-black, and she lit the lamp. Looking at herself in the mirror, she saw sunburned cheeks and ratty hair, a different person from the former belle of the ball, but at least she was trying to save what was left of her inheritance, instead of whining and crying.

She undressed, folding her dirty clothing over the chair. Naked except for her underwear, her smooth supple skin glowing in the light of the lamp, she kneeled at her cot and said her prayers.

"Dear Lord," she whispered, "please help me get my herd to Abilene, and please keep the Indians away."

She blew out the lamp, crawled into bed, and closed her eyes. In moments she was fast asleep.

It was two o'clock in the morning, and Lobo crept toward the herd, his legs bent and nose close to the ground. The rich smell of meat, the most delicious fragrance imaginable, had lured him out of his cave.

He was hungry, and he wasn't alone. Other lobos also detected blood, and were converging on the herd with him. They'd attack in a pack, bring down one fat steer, and gorge themselves on his dripping flesh.

Lobo was the leader, and electricity crackled his veins as he moved upwind from the herd, passing a pile of rocks that once had slept beneath an alluvial sea. To his left was a patch of greasewood, and he veered away because it might conceal deadly snakes, scorpions, or birds that swooped out of the sky and carried you away in their razor talons.

Lobo looked up, but no birds were there. He came to a stop, and the other lobos gathered around, mouths open and tongues hanging, gazing at the juicy creatures straight ahead. Lobo glanced at his compadres, and their eyes danced with excitement. It was the best sport they knew.

Lobo crept nearer, his chin scraping the ground. The tactic was get close as possible, then attack swiftly and mercilessly. Slithering through the grass, they heard a sound in the distance, and froze motionless in the moonlight. It was a cowboy approaching out of the clumps of mesquite and prickly pear.

The cowboy was John Stone, asleep in his saddle. He was on night duty, riding around the herd, while Joe Little Bear, a half-breed Sioux, rode in the opposite direction. A cow made a sudden bleating sound, and Stone woke suddenly, looked at the cattle, and many were standing, scanning the hills, nervous about something.

There was only one thing to do. It was ridiculous, but no less an authority than Duke Truscott himself had ordered him to *sing* to the cattle when they became restless, because the sound of a cowboy's voice was supposed to be reassuring. Stone opened his mouth and tried to yodel, but sounded like a prairie chicken in its death throes. The cowboys said yodeling calmed the cattle more than anything else, and Stone hoped to refine his technique as the drive progressed.

Stone patted Tomahawk's mane, while Tomahawk smelled the faint trace of lobos. Tomahawk's large luminescent eyes raked over the prairie, and he knew the lobos probably would strike sometime that night, but there was nothing he could do.

Every cowboy reserved his best horse for night duty, and Tomahawk was a black stallion with good lines, lots of bottom, and keen eyes. He wouldn't run into a tree, or trip over a gopher hole in the dark. Stone came to steers and cows lying on their sides, wheezing through their great black nostrils. Drooping in his saddle, Stone was weary from four or five hours of sleep per night. He'd learned that a cattle drive was similar to a military campaign, and the only way to survive was get as much sleep as possible.

Slipchuck had told him the cowboy remedy for sleepiness. He took out his bag of tobacco, placed a pinch on his tongue, and wet it thoroughly. Then he rubbed the tobacco juice into his eyes. It stung like fire, and nearly blinded him, but woke him up. At least he wouldn't fall off his horse and land on his head.

A figure loomed out of the night: Joe Little Bear, a husky figure atop a roan pony, wearing a black leather vest over his bare chest, the tooth of a panther hung from a rawhide strand around his neck. His black hair hung to his shoulders, and he carried a long knife in a sheath attached to his belt. The scuttlebutt said his mother had been white, captured by Sioux Indians when she was small, and his father had been an Indian chief.

"Cattle back there are spooked," Stone said. "Something's up."

"Wolves," Joe Little Bear replied, his Indian blood telling him what was up, his large, hooked nose sniffing at the faint scent.

"Ever been in a stampede?" Stone asked.

"A few." Joe Little Bear looked at the knife stuck into Stone's boot. "Apache," he said. "Where'd you get it?"

"Had an Apache friend once."

Joe Little Bear spat at the ground. "Apaches are killers!"

"They say the same about the Sioux."

"I am a mongrel dog, but I have sharp teeth. Do you know how to use that knife, John Stone?"

"If I didn't know how to use it, I wouldn't carry it."

Joe Little Bear pulled out his own knife, and moonbeams rolled along the blade. "Want to fight, John Stone?"

"Up to you."

Joe Little Bear laughed and put his spurs to his horse's flanks. The roan plodded away, and Stone was left alone at the edge of the herd. Stone urged Tomahawk forward, and they continued to circle, while in the distance he could hear Joe Little Bear singing an old Sioux melody to the skitterish longhorns.

The lobos waited silently until the riders passed out of earshot, and then moved forward silently over dirt and tufts of grass. They were crazed with food lust, and could almost taste the blood on their tongues.

They wanted to get their teeth into the meat, and if it twisted and fought, so much the better. Soundlessly they advanced toward the edge of the herd, and came to a stop. Now it was time to attack, and the first one in ate the liver. Lobo raised himself off the ground slowly, his tiny eyes like chips of ice in the night. He saw the fat steer sleeping, facing toward him.

Lobo sprang off the ground, and the race was on! An old bull, on guard at the edge of the herd, raised his chin and looked in their direction. He bellowed mightily, and jumped to his feet. The rest of the herd was up two seconds later. They saw the wolves, leapt around, and fled, to escape the vicious sharp teeth snapping at their heels. The herd gathered speed and rumbled across the valley, heading toward the moon.

Stone, dozing again in his saddle, was awakened by an incredible roar. He opened his eyes, and was horrified to see the entire herd of cattle heading directly toward him.

Tomahawk spun around quickly and plunged into the night, while Stone tucked in his knees and held on. Behind him he heard the most fearsome sound since the war. He flashed on an image of himself trampled to death beneath twelve thousand hooves, and urged Tomahawk on.

Tomahawk stretched forward and kicked hard, clods of dirt flying into the air behind him, and the cattle bellowed in terror; Tomahawk could hear their great lungs sucking wind. Stone turned around in his saddle and looked at the thundering herd.

It was a beast with a thousand eyes, hooting and mooing, horns flashing and popping in the moonlight, hurtling at top speed across the prairie, but Tomahawk could outrun any longhorn who ever lived. He stretched forward smoothly and carried Stone from the path of the stampeding half-crazed bovines.

Now the herd was thirty yards to Stone's right, running wildly over the grass and stones. Truscott's orders were to stay with them, and that's what Stone intended to do. Tomahawk galloped alongside the cattle, heading for the front rank.

The sound reminded Stone of cavalry charges during the war, and he crouched low in his saddle. Wind pushed back the brim of his old Confederate campaign hat, and he turned to gaze at moonlight glowing dully on the rippling backs of the cattle. They were a massive undulating brown carpet on a rampage, and Stone had a mad thought: *If a man were agile enough, he might walk on that carpet and live to tell the tale.* But something wasn't quite right, and it bothered him. He looked up at the North Star, and realized the herd was headed directly toward the encampment! He pulled out his gun and fired three warning shots, as Tomahawk sped over the prairie, following the thundering, mooing, drooling mass of fear-crazed brutes through the endless night.

Only one steer had been left behind, his rear legs collapsed underneath him, the hamstring torn away. This was the fat one selected by the lobos, and they ripped bleeding chunks of flesh off his body with their sharp fangs.

The steer fought back bravely, trying to gore the lobos with his horns, but they danced nimbly out of his way. A bold lobo lacerated the steer's foreleg hamstring, and the heavy creature fell on his face. Lobo snarled and lunged forward, tearing a gash in the steer's throat. The steer struggled, as blood spouted out of the wound, and the steer felt sharp teeth sink into his tender haunches. He took a deep breath, and Lobo darted in again, ripping out half his tongue.

Blood burbled out of the steer's mouth, and a lobo chewed off his ear, while another sank a tooth into his eye. The steer fainted from loss of blood, and the lobos dug into him, devouring his warm flesh. Lobo raised his snout to the heavens, howling the victory song.

Truscott was first to raise his head. A terrible clamor was on the plains, headed directly toward them.

"Stampede!" He pulled his Colt and fired two warning shots, but everybody was up before the second left the barrel. Truscott and the cowboys ran toward the remuda, but then Truscott remembered Cassandra, and veered toward her tent.

She poked her head outside, wearing only her underwear. Had somebody said *Stampede*?

"Hurry up!" Truscott hollered. "There ain't much time!"

She heard the pounding and trampling, her eyes widened, and she charged out of the tent, then realized she wasn't completely dressed. Turning, she dived back inside and put on her clothes quickly in the dark.

"Supposed to sleep with yer clothes *on!*" Truscott hollered.

She pulled on her boots, dropped her hat on her head, and ran toward him. Truscott grabbed her hand, dragging her toward the remuda.

"They're leaving the chuck wagon!" Cassandra protested.

"No time!" Truscott replied.

Everybody's night horse was saddled, in case of emergencies such as the one occurring at that moment. The cowboys and vaqueros already were speeding away, as Cassandra untied her palomino mare, climbed into the saddle, and the mare bounded away before Cassandra was settled, but she managed to hang on. Truscott jumped onto his horse's back, and the animal neighed in terror. Truscott gave him the spurs, and the chestnut stallion sprang forward, leaping over the dead embers of the campfire, galloping away from the mighty onrushing herd.

The lobos were covered with blood from head to foot as they feasted on the dead steer. Barking and howling with glee, they ripped strands of flesh away, while their puppies were living balls of gore, digging their needle teeth into juicy steaming meat. A few feet away, Lobo lay in the bushes and chewed the steer's liver, the choicest part. This was his reward and tribute for being the lobo chief, and he reveled in the rich smelly stuff.

Every night the lobos sallied forth across the prairie; the search for meat never ended. Sometimes they returned hungry, or they ate creatures smaller than themselves, and occasionally, like tonight, cattle emerged bountifully from the heart of the lobo god.

Lobo growled with pleasure as the glistening white bones of the steer came into view, and his body disappeared into the bellies of the hungry animals.

Stone rode beside the burgeoning herd, the night wind stroking his beard. The cattle generated tremendous heat, searing his cheeks, and straight ahead, peacefully composed in the moonlight, were the chuck wagon, Cassandra's buckboard, the tent, and the fire pit. The cattle rampaged toward them, and Stone recalled his bedroll and saddlebags out there someplace. Everything would be stomped to hell in just a few moments.

He watched in morbid fascination at the cattle plowed into the chuck wagon, and it shook, tipped over, and was pushed forward by the power of the animals. Some cattle tried to get out of the way, while others slammed into it, breaking their necks. Other cattle piled on top of them, climbed over, and kept charging. Cassandra's tent went down like paper and disappeared off the face of the earth.

A figure rode toward him out of the night, and it was Truscott accompanied by Moose Roykins, Calvin Blakemore, and the *segundo*.

"Mill 'em!" Truscott shouted, riding hatless through the night, his long mustaches streaming in the wind.

Stone spurred Tomahawk, and felt the thrill of the chase. They had to shunt the longhorns to the side, working them into a mill that would force them to run in circles until they tired.

Truscott held his reins tightly and slapped them back and forth over the haunches of his chestnut stallion. The stallion rushed onward, and Moose Roykins rode behind Truscott, with the *segundo* to the left of Truscott. They saw Calvin Blakemore and Luke Duvall cut in from the right, and then, pulling ahead of them all, were Don Emilio Maldonado and his Mexican vaqueros.

They yipped and yelled, sang Mexican songs, waved their sombreros in the air. Stone could see a contest developing between Mexicans and the Americans as they rounded the first rank of cattle, and then out of the night rode Ephraim waving his lariat in the air. The cattle saw the mass of riders charging toward them, and swerved to avoid a collision.

"They turn!" Don Emilio shouted. *"Vamanos, muchachos!"*

Stone took off his hat and waved it in the air. "Come on, cows!"

The cattle were confused, and many had forgotten why they were running, but that didn't stop them. Snorting and dripping long strings of snot from their mouths and noses, they trampled over the prairie, making a wide parabola on the enormous expanse.

"We got 'em!" Truscott yelled, raising his fist in the air. "Don't let 'em get away!"

2

THE CATTLE CAME to a halt on a vast plain. Their tongues hung out, their eyes were bloodshot, and their breath came in gasps. Sullenly, they gazed at the cowboys in the wan dawn light.

Truscott called a meeting, and the cowboys gathered around, frazzled and haggard. They slouched in their saddles, and some puffed cigarettes, as Truscott gave assignments in a hoarse, tired voice.

Stone listened with a headache, and his ass hurt from the night of hard riding. It was like the war, after a big battle, but no one had been shooting at him, and no grapeshot ripped men's heads off. He figured he'd only slept three hours, but there was work to do.

Truscott ordered the vaqueros to hold the herd, several cowboys would hunt stray cattle and horses, and the rest return to the campsite to see what could be salvaged.

Cassandra was in the group that rode back to the campsite, and saw the destroyed chuck wagon. How could they get to Abilene without a chuck wagon? Her buckboard was ruined, and God only knew what happened to her tent. The ground was covered with bits of clothing and blankets. Bags of beans and barrels of flour were demolished. Splinters and chunks of wood lay everywhere. The chuck wagon wheels were smashed.

Truscott climbed down from his saddle and walked bow-legged in his leggins toward the chuck wagon. "Git the tools out!" he bellowed. "I want this rig runnin' by noon!"

Cowboys dismounted and searched for the hammer and nails. Cassandra wheeled her palomino and rode toward the spot where her tent had been pitched. She passed the trampled fire pit, and her eyes fell on dark brown leather, somebody's saddlebags. She dismounted, picked them up, and they were John Stone's. A flap had been kicked open, and out fell Stone's isinglass photo of Marie, in a bent silver frame.

Cassandra picked it up, and saw a young woman almost her mirror image, but she thought Marie's features were a little too cute, and her dress overdone with ruffles and lace. Stone had searched for her all across creation, ever since the shooting stopped at Appomattox, so she must have a redeeming quality somewhere, although Cassandra certainly couldn't see it in the picture. *Little Bitch.*

She dropped it into the saddlebags and set to work collecting the salvageable belongings of the other cowboys, as behind her the hammering began.

At noon the chuck wagon was standing. It had a certain bizarre lean, and numerous chunks of wood were missing in its superstructure. Patched with rawhide and cottonwood, the wheels had been rebuilt, and the mules recovered, dazed by the madness of three thousand crazy longhorns.

The cowboys fixed Cassandra's buckboard, while she sat on the grass near the chuck wagon and watched Ephraim build a fire. He'd found some coffee, and scraped together a few handfuls of beans. They'd live on beef mostly until they could find a town where flour and other commodities could be purchased.

Ephraim passed her a dinged tin cup filled with thick black liquid, and she raised it to her lips.

"Don't worry, Mrs. Cassandra," he said, dark eyes flashing. "We'll make it to Abilene."

"I hope you're right," she replied wearily, because she wasn't so sure.

"This is nothin'." He gestured toward the scattered herd. "We'll put it back together."

Cattle had been separated from the main herd during the stampede, and cowboys rode the endless wastes, searching for stragglers and holdouts. The hot sun baked their brains, no water was in the vicinity, and Indians could attack at any moment. The stampede had destroyed their water barrels, along with everything else.

John Stone's throat felt like sand whenever he swallowed, and his tongue was a ball of cotton. He dreamed of cool, clear water in a tall glass as he rode Tomahawk and swung his lasso, moving four steers back to the herd. He was on a massive rolling plain, and spires jutted into the distant sky.

He recalled when he'd awakened in his saddle, and seen the herd rushing toward him. For a moment he thought he'd be crushed beneath their hooves, but Tomahawk had galloped away, saving both their lives.

It reminded him of a drunken binge one night in San Antone, when he'd visited an old Gypsy hag, and she told him he was going to die young. Ever since, her curse undermined his confidence and bedeviled him at every turn. She was a fraud like all Gypsies, and how could anything besides hard work be seen in the calluses of a man's hand, but the incident ate at his innards like a gray rat, and he couldn't forget it.

His only consolation was she'd given the same prediction to Calvin Blakemore, and they figured she sold the identical bill of goods to every cowboy who visited her seedy little parlor, so they'd pay more to find out how to avoid their early funerals.

Something caught the corner of his eye. Indians at the top of a rise nearby. They numbered about twenty, lances and warbonnets silhouetted against the sky, garish war paint on their faces. He stared at them for a few moments, then Tomahawk broke into a slow trot, heading back toward the herd.

Stone turned in his saddle and looked at the Indians congregated atop the hill. He didn't feel up to a fight after chasing the herd most of the night. Were they just paying a social call? A white man couldn't expect anything good from Indians.

Stone returned to the herd and found Truscott and the other cowboys and vaqueros gathered together on their horses, checking rifles and pistols, as Truscott addressed them: "I'll do the talkin', and don't nobody shoot less'n I give the word."

Truscott and the cowboys prodded their horses and moved toward the hill that the Indians were descending slowly, while Stone surveyed the situation with the eyes of a cavalry officer. A long-range shoot-out would benefit the cowboys, because they had more rifles, but close hand-to-hand fighting was the specialty of the Indian, and they outnumbered the cowboys approximately two to one. If Stone were in charge, he'd order his men to fire warning shots, to make the Indians keep their distance.

"Look like Osage," Slipchuck said.

The Indians and cowboys moved toward each other across the sea of buffalo grass. Stone peered at the creatures from another world, their bodies painted grotesquely, wearing beads, bones, and feathers, led by a middle-aged man wearing a warbonnet and a breechclout, carrying a lance. He was followed by four lieutenants also wearing warbonnets, and then came the mass of warriors with only a few feathers sticking out of their headbands.

The Indians and cowboys approached each other, and the Indian chief held up the palm of his hand.

"How, John," he said. "Ten *wo-haw*."

Wo-haw was the Indian word for a cow or steer, and they called all cowboys John, an irony not missed by John Stone. Truscott raised his forefinger in the air. "One *wo-haw*."

The chief looked angry, and mumbled with his lieutenants, while the warriors brandished their lances and bows and shouted insults.

The chief turned to Truscott again. "This our land. You go through, you pay ten *wo-haw*."

"One *wo-haw*."

"You not go through."

Truscott leaned over his saddle horn. "We got rifles, and my men are brave warriors. If we fight, women will wail in their tepees tonight. Take one *wo-haw* and go in peace."

The chief conferred with his advisers, then turned to Truscott and said, "Four *wo-haw*."

"One *wo-haw*."

"You insult me!"

"I want to give you one *wo-haw*. Yer women and babies will fill their bellies tonight."

"Not fill bellies with one *wo-haw*. Give two *wo-haw*."

"One *wo-haw*. Nice fat one. Taste good."

The chief raised his hand and shouted, and his warriors turned around, riding away from the cowboys. The warriors gathered around the chief, and a heated discussion ensued. Stone thought they might attack, and the cowboys should take cover. Touching his heels to Tomahawk's withers, he advanced to Truscott's side.

"Don't you think we should fall back and set up a skirmish line, Ramrod?"

Truscott looked at him as if he were a freak. "Get the hell back where you was!"

"If they attack, we can fight better from a skirmish line."

"They ain't a-gonna attack, you damn fool. Git out'n my road."

Stone returned to his position near Blakemore, Duvall, and Slipchuck, his closest friends on the drive, and then faced the Indians, who argued among themselves for several minutes. Finally they re-formed and rode back toward the cowboys, led by their chief. He held up his hand, and the warriors stopped behind him. The chief looked at Truscott and said with as much dignity as he could muster, "One *wo-haw*."

"One *wo-haw* it is." Truscott turned to the Mexican vaquero behind him and winked. "Cut out the best steer you can find!"

The vaquero's name was Pedro, and he slapped the backs of his fingers against the brim of his sombrero. Wheeling his horse, he rode back to the herd. The Indians moved away and dismounted, sitting cross-legged on the ground. Stone rolled a cigarette as he scrutinized them. They were proud men reduced to begging for cattle on their shrunken ancestral domain, and how they must hate the white cowboys.

Pedro returned a short while later with a spavined half-blind cow whose ribs were showing. The cowboys sat their horses as Pedro drove the cow toward the Indians. The cow was befuddled by the sudden change in plans, and saw the Indians rush toward her, knives in hands. She turned to run, but then they were all over her, blades flashing in the sunlight. She collapsed onto the ground, and they slit her from top to bottom, pulled out her warm entrails, and devoured them raw, blood dripping down their chins.

Late in the afternoon, Ephraim arrived with the repaired chuck wagon, followed by Cassandra in her buckboard. Ephraim built a fire, and the cowboys returned to the encampment for supper, driving a steer before them.

They butchered the steer much like the Indians, and slaked their thirst with its blood. Slipchuck carried a battered tin cup full of maroon fluid to Cassandra. "Have a drink, boss lady!"

"Is that what I think it is?"

"Fresh blood!"

"I'm not that thirsty."

"If you don't want it, ma'am, mind if I take a sip?"

"Help yourself," she replied, and shuddered as she watched Slipchuck guzzling the blood; she felt she was back in some prehistoric cave. Ephraim cut off a big chunk of fat and carried it to the chuck wagon, where he hacked it to pieces and threw some into a big skillet over the fire.

The fat sizzled as it hit the pan. Some cowboys dragged a haunch of steer toward the fire and dropped it onto Ephraim's cutting board. Ephraim pulled his long butcher knife out of its sheath, tested its edge with his thumb, ran the stone over the blade a few times, and proceeded to carve thick steaks. Cassandra watched muscles ripple on Ephraim's back as he worked.

The other cowboys gathered around the fire, holding their banged-up tin plates and cups, and grinned like dogs. Ephraim threw steaks on the skillet, and a ball of smoke rose into the sky. The cowboys lined up with their tin plates, and the sun sank behind basins and bald knobs in the west, giving the sky a reddish glow.

Cassandra picked up her tin plate and walked toward the front of the line, since she was boss lady. The cowboys stepped back to make room for her, and she felt the intensity of their eyes. They could do anything they wanted to her, and the *segundo* stood at the head of the line, a crooked smile on his face.

Cassandra moved in front of him, and could hear the *segundo* breathing noisily behind her. Ephraim speared a steak with his long fork and dropped it on Cassandra's plate. The fragrant meat overflowed the edges, and Cassandra carried it to her buckboard, got on her knees, and sliced off a piece.

The line moved forward and Ephraim threw steaks on plates. Stone was midway in the line, and when his turn came, Ephraim placed a steak on his plate with such force that the steak fell off and dropped to the ground. Ephraim ignored it, and plopped a steak on the next plate. The line kept moving. Stone looked at his steak on the ground. Ephraim had done it on purpose, but there was nothing Stone could do. The fight, when it came, would have to be in solitude, so no one would stop it. Stone tramped to the end of the line and worked his way forward again. Ephraim turned to him and said gruffly, "No more."

"Cut me another steak."

The other cowboys moved away from the fire. Ephraim looked at Stone and said curtly, "Cut it yourself!"

Ephraim walked toward the wagon tongue with his plate. Stone pulled out his Apache knife, bent over, and looked at the steer's carcass. The choicest cuts were gone, but he was able to slice off a decent chunk of sirloin.

He threw the steak into the skillet, and fat spit into the air. During the war he'd lived outdoors for nearly all of five years, and this wasn't the first time he'd cooked over a campfire. He dropped the steak onto his plate, and carried it to a spot near Blakemore and Duvall.

"Knew I shouldn't've signed up for this drive," said Duvall, who looked like a ferret, chewing steadily. "Things is gonna git nasty around here, we don't run into water soon."

"Got to be water someplace," Blakemore replied, his old Yankee forage cap slanted over his eyes. "This ain't no desert. If we dug a hole we'd hit water."

"You could dig clear to China, and not find a drop. I seen a whole wagon train full of dead folks, their mouths open and their tongues black. No water."

Ephraim boiled water he'd found at the bottom of a stove-in barrel, and floating amid the bubbles were leaves, grass, and twigs. "Made some range coffee for you fellers!" he said. "Ain't as good as the real thang, but it's the realest we got!"

Ephraim always acted dumb and servile to avoid trouble with the white cowboys, but was a powder keg ready to explode, Stone knew. The cowboys lined up in front of the fire, and Stone walked toward the end of the line. Cassandra took her place at the front again, and Ephraim ladled his range coffee into her cup. The line passed along, and Cassandra stepped out of the way, raising the cup to her lips.

It had a strong bitter taste, but she drank it anyway, while worrying about bedding down with the cowboys, because God only knew what they'd do close together on the ground. But she didn't dare move too far from them either, because of

Indians. *Maybe I'll sleep in the wagon, and I won't have to worry about snakes.*

Stone approached Ephraim, who jerked his wrist suddenly, splashing hot scalding brew onto Stone's hands.

"Sorry."

Stone didn't let the pain show, but realized he'd have to be careful whenever he came near Ephraim. "I'll pour my own," he said.

Ephraim stepped backward, and Stone filled his cup. Sometimes he worried Ephraim would poison him, so he never ate or drank anything that didn't come from a common pot. He sipped the liquid, far different from hot black coffee, but better than nothing.

"What is this pisswater!" shouted the *segundo*, pouring his range coffee onto the ground. "Goddamn burrhead—what the hell you tryin' to give us!"

Ephraim went into his dumb nigra routine. "Just my mammy's range coffee, boss. Thought you might like it, since there ain't no real coffee."

The *segundo* stomped toward him. "Who told you thet you know how to *think*, burrhead?"

"You don't like it, you don't drink it, boss."

"I don't like it, but you sass me, I'll throw you right in thet pot!"

Ephraim shuffled and smiled. He didn't dare fight a white man and win in Texas, because they'd hang him from the nearest tree, or burn him alive. Stone watched carefully. *The son of a bitch knows how to hold it in.*

Cassandra didn't like the *segundo*'s bad manners, and didn't understand why Truscott hadn't reprimanded him. She wanted to say something herself, but the incident passed, and the *segundo* slouched off toward his spot of ground. "Goddamn burrhead thinks he owns the world."

He dropped to the ground and rolled a cigarette. Slipchuck shuffled by and sat near him. He leaned toward the *segundo* and said softly, "I wouldn't talk to him that way if I were you."

The *segundo* scowled at him. "Get the hell away from me, you old fart, or I'll throw you in the pot with the burrhead."

Slipchuck arose and walked away from the *segundo*, heading for the range coffee. He filled up his cup, smiled respectfully to

Ephraim, and sat on the ground next to his saddle.

Slipchuck was scared to death of Ephraim. One night, back at the Triangle Spur, he'd peered through a crack in the window of Ephraim's room, and seen Ephraim seated on the floor, playing with beads, bones, candles, and skulls. Ephraim had worn white robes and a strange blue African turban, and chanted a weird melody in a strange language.

Slipchuck's momma had warned him about the old hoodoo religion. "Stay away from them nigras," she said. "They'll turn you into a turtle, or a frog, or maybe even a fly."

Slipchuck still believed what his momma told him, and knew the *segundo*'s days were numbered. Ephraim was a hoodoo priest in his secret spare time, and the *segundo* had been insulting him steadily ever since Slipchuck was hired. Slipchuck had warned the *segundo*, and could do no more.

He didn't dare tell the cowboys what he'd seen, because Ephraim would surely kill him. He wouldn't even tell John Stone, his pard.

He looked across the campsite and saw the ex-cavalry officer fast asleep, his plate of half-eaten steak beside him. Stone's chest rose and fell steadily with his breathing, and the sight of him made Slipchuck realize he was tired too. He stretched out and lay his weary head on his saddle. *Goddamn, what a day. Crazy fuckin' cows, crazy injuns, crazy* segundo. *I'm the only sane man on this drive.*

The sun had set and cowboys crawled beneath their ragged blankets, while those who had no blankets cuddled against the ground. Cassandra climbed into the wagon and lay on the hard floorboards, with a pile of dirty clothing for her pillow. It wasn't too uncomfortable if she stayed on her back, but even in that position her spine was bent out of shape and her hips hurt. She'd get through the night somehow, but what about the herd? If the cattle stampeded again, they might get away, and if they got away, she was ruined.

She hadn't said her prayers, but was too tired to climb onto her knees. "Please, Lord," she whispered, "don't let the cowboys rape me."

The cattle were thirsty, and moaned pathetically in the moonlight. Some wanted to go back to the last water, and others wanted to look for new water. They couldn't sleep, hadn't

STAMPEDE

forgotten the lobos, and were thoroughly spooked. It wouldn't take much to set them off.

The Osage warriors appeared on the crest of a hogback, in the light of the full moon. The feathers in their headdresses pointed at the stars, and they carried bows and spears, and their faces still were covered with war paint. They were led by the same chief who'd begged for cattle earlier in the day, but now their numbers had grown to more than fifty battle-hardened warriors. The cowboys had given them a sick old cow, the height of contempt and disrespect.

Their opportunity to pass in peace was over. Now they must pay. The warriors came to the bottom of the rise and the cattle were straight ahead, turned in their direction, sniffing. The old chief raised his war lance in the air, and moved it forward.

The warriors shrieked, kicked the flanks of their horses, and their horses sprang toward the cattle. Screaming at the tops of their lungs, the warriors raced across the plain, aiming their arrows at the cattle.

One moment the night was silent, and the next it was filled with a tornado. The Indians charged into the cattle, shooting arrows into their thick hides, and the animals mooed as they crashed bleeding to the ground, to be trampled by other cattle.

At the campsite, the earth trembled. This time Joe Little Bear was the first to open his eyes. He jumped to his feet and screamed: *"Stampede!"*

The cowboys only had slept a few hours, but leapt up with alacrity, guns in their hands, cattle heading their way again. The cowboys turned and ran toward the remuda, jumped on their horses, and were off.

John Stone rode a hundred yards before he realized Cassandra wasn't among them, which meant she was still sleeping soundly in her wagon. Stone pulled Tomahawk's head back toward the campsite, and Tomahawk balked. Stone slapped him over the head. "We got to get the boss lady!"

Tomahawk broke into a reluctant gallop, angling toward the campsite, while Cassandra stirred on the buckboard. Something was making it shake, and she wished it would go away. Yawning, she rolled over onto her side, and felt wooden planks against her tender hip. The pain prodded her to alertness, and she became aware of galloping hooves.

Raising her head, she gazed at the herd careening toward her out of the night, and nearly fainted. She heard hoofbeats behind her, and spun around. John Stone and Tomahawk galloped toward the buckboard. Cassandra was in shock. Stone pulled back his reins, Tomahawk raised his front hooves into the air, and Stone wrapped his arm around Cassandra's waist. He picked her up, dropped her astraddle Tomahawk, and the sleek black stallion bounded away.

Tomahawk felt the added weight on his back, and exerted himself to the maximum as he galloped out of the path of the marauding cattle. Cassandra looked at the ominous dark mass rolling by, hooting and mooing, moonlight glinting on their horns.

"They nearly killed me," she whispered, trying to understand how such a thing could happen to a belle of New Orleans.

"You say something?" he asked.

She patted the horse's mane. "Thank you, Tomahawk."

Stone was looking back at the herd rumbling in bestial panic through the night, and saw Indians riding among the longhorns, sliding up and down the sides of their horses, firing arrows into the cattle from all positions. The longhorns crashed to the ground as the Indians charged forward, and each dead steer or cow was money out of Cassandra's purse.

Tomahawk galloped into the mesquite, leaving the stampede behind. Stone became aware of Cassandra's body rubbing against him, and could smell the fragrance of her hair. She wore a thin dress and he a thin shirt, and their mutual warmth passed through the material. But fifty yards away lunatic Indians were screaming ancient brain-shriveling cries.

Cassandra held the saddle horn to keep from falling off, and Stone wrapped his arm around her waist to steady her. She could feel his chest against her back, and his body was practically wrapped around her.

Stone pulled back the reins when they were far from the Indians. He and Cassandra rested against each other for a few seconds, feeling the press of each other's bodies.

He climbed out of the saddle, then helped her to the ground. She looked in the direction of the distant roar, and returned to her worry about the herd. "I hope we have something left in the morning," she said.

"Injuns can't kill 'em all."

"Indians make life hell for everybody out here."

"We make life hell for them too."

He looked at her upturned nose, just like Marie's. "A herd of cattle nearly trampled you to death. Sleep with one eye open."

"How do you sleep with one eye open?"

"You'll have to learn, because if you don't, you're liable to wake up one morning in an Indian encampment, and you'll have a new husband. He might beat you once in a while, but it's better than being scalped."

Before she realized what she was saying, the words were out of her mouth. "Maybe you should sleep near me, to wake me in case of trouble."

"Sleep with all of us. We'll take care of you, and I'm sure nobody'll bother you."

"I'm afraid I don't have your confidence in that pack of cutthroats, thieves, and drunkards."

"Most of them would gladly die for you. They proved it at the ranch, didn't they?"

"Sometimes I think they saved me so they can torment me."

"They want you to join in the fun with them."

"The fun of raping me? Well, I'm sorry, but that's not something I look forward to."

They waited in silence for several minutes, as Cassandra calculated her losses, and Stone gazed at the stars. He saw the Big Dipper, the North Star, and then looked at his favorite constellation, Orion the Warrior, belted with stars, carrying a sword of stars. To Stone he symbolized every soldier who'd ever gone down fighting, plus the ones who'd survived and become lost, wandering freebooters like himself.

"We'd better start looking for the others," he said.

"I'll ride in back this time."

Stone lifted and placed her on the rear of the saddle. Then he climbed in front, and there was nowhere for her to put her hands except around his waist. There was no flab on him; he was solid as a mountain. He drew one of his Colts, and examined the mesquite. From far off he could hear the herd still moving across the prairie.

"You know how to shoot a gun?" he asked.

"Of course I know how to shoot a gun. I'm not as useless as everybody thinks."

"Pull out my other gun, and get ready to shoot."

She yanked the Colt out of his left holster, transferred it to her right hand, held it tightly, and pulled back the hammer.

"Don't shoot me by mistake," he said.

He was treating her like a fool again, and she wondered what she had to do to make the men respect her. "I have very good vision," she replied dryly. "You can rest assured I won't shoot you."

"People get flustered and shoot the wrong person."

"I don't get flustered."

Something huge lay on the grass ahead of them, and as they drew closer, Cassandra saw a steer with arrows sticking out of its body. Ten yards later they saw another. Stone and Cassandra followed the path of the stampede, while dead cattle sprawled endlessly before them, each a financial setback for Cassandra. More dead cattle loomed ahead, and her spirits sank lower. The herd was gone. *I'm flustered,* she thought. *I'm flustered as hell.*

Tomahawk stopped and pricked up his ears.

"What's the matter?" Stone asked.

Tomahawk peered straight ahead. Danger.

Stone pulled Tomahawk's head to the side, and they moved behind some cottonwoods. Stone and Cassandra parted the branches and leaves and peered at Indians returning with Cassandra's buckboard. Unmounted warriors dashed among the carcasses, skinning them with deft, sure strokes of their sharp knives. They tore great sheets of skin off the dead animals and stacked the hides on the buckboard that rolled among them. Chanting their victory song, the Indians plundered the stampede ground, moonlight flashing on their cruel blades.

3

STONE AND CASSANDRA caught up to Truscott and the other cowboys shortly after dawn, and received the bad news.

One vaquero and one cowboy had been killed in the stampede. They lay stretched on the ground, battered by cattles' hooves, and not far away, the other cowboys sat with grim expressions and pallid faces, smoking cigarettes. Beyond them, on a flat mesa, approximately one half of the original herd grazed peacefully.

Truscott sat with his arms hugging his knees, staring vacantly at the cattle. Cassandra wanted to tell him to put the cowboys to work finding lost cattle, but thought she'd better not meddle in his business. She sat on the ground among them and performed calculations on her notepad. If she ended up in Abilene with fifteen hundred head of cattle, she'd be able to pay off her creditors and cowboys, and then she'd be on her own with only a few hundred dollars profit, if she were lucky.

Stone sat near her and rolled a cigarette. Nobody said anything. A breeze rustled the prairie grass, and buzzards swarmed in the distance, devouring dead cattle.

Truscott took off his hat and ran his fingers through his sandy graying hair. "Wa'al, the longer we stay here, the harder it'll be to round up strays. We better git started."

They heard the voice of Joe Little Bear. "Maybe you should've offered 'em more'n one sick cow, Ramrod."

Truscott turned toward him and scowled. "I don't remember askin' fer yer opinion, injun. They would've attacked anyways, because that's the way injuns are."

Joe Little Bear said no more, but Cassandra's curiosity was provoked. "What's this about giving them a sick cow?"

Nobody said a word. Cassandra waited patiently for an answer, but silence descended like a black cloud over the cowboys. They treated her as if she didn't exist, and she was getting sick of it. She rose to her feet. "I just asked a question!" she said, and turned to Truscott. "What about that sick cow, Ramrod?"

Truscott reluctantly explained the bargaining session in a deadpan voice, then spat at the ground.

"Now let me get this straight," she said. "Are you telling me if you gave them a few decent steers, this might not've happened?"

"That's not what I'm sayin', ma'am. It's what *you're* sayin'. The stampede would've happened no matter what we done, but the worst thing is show weakness to an injun."

"Next time we hold negotiations with Indians, I should be there."

Truscott blew his nose with his thumb and finger. "If that's the way you think, you can start a-lookin' fer another ramrod."

Truscott walked toward his horse, and Cassandra followed him, realizing she'd punctured his absurd masculine vanity. She couldn't let him get away, even if he'd made an error of judgment. She trailed after him as he headed toward his horse, and she wracked her brain for something to say. But she couldn't beg, because that would make everything worse, and then it occurred to her that his vanity was his weakest spot. She put a taunting note into her voice as she said derisively, "I thought I heard you say once, when you take a man's money, you ride for the brand."

"You ain't no man."

"The money spends the same no matter who gives it to you."

Truscott reached his horse, placed his foot in the stirrup, and turned to Cassandra. "What money?" he asked sarcastically.

"The money you'll get when you reach Abilene."

"We ain't goin' to Abilene, unless you butt out of my business."

"If any important decisions have to be made concerning my herd, I want to be in on them."

Truscott removed his foot from the stirrup and stared at her. "I don't take orders from women."

"You signed on this cattle drive."

"We'd be okay, if the boss lady stayed out of our road."

Again they heard the deep voice of Joe Little Bear. "Boss lady is right. You give sick old cow—what you expect? It was slap in face to old chief in front of warriors."

"What the hell do you know about it?" Truscott spun toward Joe Little Bear. "Maybe you're in cahoots with 'em."

Joe Little Bear stepped forward, a blank expression on his face. Truscott moved away from his horse and spread his legs, his hand hovering over his Remington. Cassandra stepped between them.

"Out of the way!" Truscott hollered.

Cassandra was getting mad. First the Indians, then the stampede, and now this. "We've got work to do!" she yelled. "I hired professional cowmen!"

"The ramrod say he's sorry, or I kill him,' Joe Little Bear replied.

"Like hell you will!" Cassandra said. "Your job is to round up lost cattle! Now get on your horse and go after them!

In 1500 moons. Joe Little Bear had never heard a squaw tell a warrior to get on his horse. Puzzled, he grumbled something, turned away, and headed in a sulk toward his horse. Cassandra faced Truscott angrily. "What're you waiting for, Ramrod—a written invitation?"

Truscott climbed into his saddle, held the reins in one hand, and issued orders to the men, his voice deadly calm. This matter wasn't closed.

One group hunted cattle, another held the herd, a third recovered their belongings, and a fourth buried the dead. Cassandra stayed behind with the burial party.

They only had one shovel, and it was bent grotesquely. Cassandra sat nearby, sucking a pebble to alleviate thirst, but no matter how hard she sucked, her mouth remained parched. There had to be water out there someplace. Other herds had made it to Abilene, and so would hers.

Moose Roykins, the Canadian lumberjack, approached her nervously. He was heavyset, thick around the middle, and his pants rode low on his hips, the crotch nearly down to his knees. "We was wonderin' if you wanted to say a prayer before we dropped the boys in the hole."

Cassandra walked to the grave. Her Bible had been trampled into the dust along with everything else she owned. Stopping at the edge of the deep yawning hole, she clasped her hands together and bowed her head. The cowboys removed their hats and stood solemnly. The corpses on the ground looked up with dead eyes at the sun they'd see no more.

"Lord," Cassandra said, "please accept the souls of these two brave men into your loving care." What else was there to say? "Forgive their sins and remember their kindness. Ashes to ashes and dust to dust. Praise be the Lord."

She stepped back, and cowboys threw the dead bodies into the common grave, where they'd be pardners forever. Cassandra walked away, hearing the shovel behind her. The sun rose in the azure sky, and puffy white clouds drifted from the north. The cowboys filled the grave with dirt and packed a mound of rocks over it, to keep predators away. Moose Roykins hammered a crude cottonwood cross tied with rawhide into the ground. The cowboys walked toward their horses, and Cassandra climbed onto her palomino. She followed the cowboys back to the herd, and when they were halfway to their destination, she turned and looked at the cross sitting forlornly atop the grave.

The cross would disappear and grass cover the grave. Settlers or other cowboys would pass this way and have no inkling of what had occurred. Two young men trampled to death, and the prairie rolled forever.

It took two days to gather the herd, and when the cowboys were finished, Truscott rode through and made a rough count. Meanwhile, Cassandra sprawled beneath a cottonwood tree, her mouth dry and a sore on her upper lip. Two of her cowboys had found a stream a few miles to the north, and she visualized nice cool water to drink, and a real bath, as Truscott approached.

"Only lost 'bout a hundred and fifty," Truscott said. "Not as bad as I thought."

She performed the calculation in her mind. One hundred fifty head of cattle were worth thirty-three hundred dollars in Abilene. "It's bad enough, Ramrod."

"Maybe we can find somebody else's strays on our way north and make up the difference."

"This is the Triangle Spur, not a gang of cattle rustlers."

"Everybody does it."

"We're not everybody."

She saw his jaw muscles working and knew he was getting mad, but she couldn't let him ride roughshod over her. "Mr. Truscott, I'm tired of hanging around, doing nothing. Isn't there some way I can help?"

A craggy smile appeared on Truscott's face. "Why don't you ask the cook?"

"He doesn't need any help, but you do. You lost two of your men. Maybe I can help fill in."

Truscott turned away and held his sunburned hand over his face as his body was wracked with laughter. Cassandra went red to the roots of her hair, and ground her teeth together in frustration. Truscott symbolized everything she hated about men, their constant cruelty and mocking condescension.

"Sorry, ma'am," he said, struggling to regain control of himself. "Couldn't he'p it. Ain't been gittin' much sleep."

"Give me a job, Ramrod. If I can't do it, I'll shut my mouth and never bother you again."

"Well," Truscott said, "when a new man without 'sperience is hired, he rides the drag. Report to John Stone. He'll break you in, and we'll see if you can handle it."

Truscott walked to his horse, and Cassandra took off her battered cowboy hat, wiped her forehead with the back of her arm, then returned the hat to her head. Filthy and sweaty, she climbed into the saddle and pulled the reins to the side. She could see the herd in the distance, a long black snake winding across the plain, and at its rear was a huge cloud of dust, the drag.

"Let's go to work, Petunia," she said to her palomino mare as she rode toward the murky, billowing dust ball that followed the herd like the plague.

John Stone rode through the midst of it, his black bandanna tied around his nose and mouth. He was on Buckshot, an old cowhorse who'd seen better days. Buckshot didn't like the drag either, and Stone had to hold him steady, otherwise he'd drift to one side in an effort to get away.

To ride the drag all the way to Abilene seemed his destiny. He was a green cowboy, like a recruit in the Army, and had to work his way up to flanker or point man. He didn't want to eat dust for the rest of his life.

The same cattle were on the drag every day. The longhorns might mix while grazing or sleeping, but the herd had a distinct hierarchy and every cow and steer knew its place. In front were young strong ones, while the blind, lame, and lazy were on the drag.

A cow with a heel problem slowed and fell behind the pace. Stone spurred Buckshot, which galloped toward the cow. Stone slapped the cow on the rump with his lasso. "Move it out, cow."

The cow groped forward, a string of saliva stretching from her lower lip. The drag was slower than the rest of the herd, which meant cowboys on the drag finished work last.

Stone heard approaching hoofbeats—Cassandra atop her palomino mare, her red bandanna over her face, a patina of dust on her clothing. She pulled Petunia alongside Buckshot, and mumbled through her bandanna. "From now on I'm riding the drag. Do you think you could sell me one of your guns?"

He unstrapped one of his gunbelts. "Don't shoot yourself by mistake."

There it was again, that nasty male condescension. She felt like hitting him over the head with his gun, but strapped it on and tied the rawhide strands at the bottom to her leg. "Truscott said you'd break me in. Tell me what to do."

"What about twenty dollars for the gun?"

"I'll pay you in Abilene. Now tell me what we do on the drag."

"We stop cattle from running away, and there goes one now. You might as well handle it."

She looked at the steer and wrinkled her nose. "How?"

"Ride up to him and tell him to get his ass moving. Personally, I think you ought to ride in front with the ramrod, and take in the scenery."

"Stone," she said, "I'm able to do my share."

She pulled Petunia away from Stone and rode toward the steer. It was covered with sores and flies, but was worth twenty-two dollars in Abilene. "Get moving!" she shouted.

The steer looked at her and didn't budge.

"Come on, now! I'm not fooling with you, dammit!"

"Hit him with your lasso!" Stone said.

She held her lasso in her right hand and maneuvered Petunia behind the steer. "Move!" she hollered, and whacked the steer's buttocks.

"Give 'im another!" Stone said.

Cassandra yelled at the steer and smacked him hard. To her amazement, the steer grunted and turned toward the herd. Her lasso whistled through the air and landed on the steer's hindquarters again, and he picked up his pace. Cassandra looked at Stone, and he saluted.

The steer caught up with the herd and loped along with his snout near the ground. Cassandra adjusted her red bandanna, pulled her hat low over her eyes, and rode the drag to Abilene.

At the stream that night, Stone saw near the chuck wagon a pile of barely recognizable personal belongings recovered after the stampede. Cowboys and vaqueros, on their hands and knees, picked through it, searching for lost items.

Old burnished brass gleamed in the middle of the mess, and Stone leaned over, picking up his squashed and scarred saddlebags. They were made of tough cowhide, and he carried them to a solitary spot, then kneeled and opened a flap.

His spare clothing was pulverized. Shredded tobacco was everywhere. His fingers touched something hard, and he pulled out his photograph of Marie.

The frame was bent in three places, but the photograph had survived. He straightened the frame carefully over a rock, then held Marie up to the moonlight. Why was it, after five long years, he couldn't forget her? How could her memory dig into his brain so deeply?

Stone heard Cassandra's voice on the other side of the campsite. "I'm going to take a bath in the stream thataway," she said, pointing. "You cowboys stay away, hear?"

Truscott spat a wad of tobacco juice on the ground. "You'd better take a guard. Might be injuns out there."

Slipchuck jumped to his feet. "I'll go!"

"Don't need a guard," Cassandra replied, drawing her six-gun. "If anything moves out there, I'll shoot his lights out."

"Suit yerself," Truscott said with a shrug.

She holstered the gun and walked toward the water.

She'd been dreaming of this bath ever since they left the Triangle Spur. Never had she gone so long without washing. She thought of cool, clear water on her skin. A good bath would improve her outlook.

Before her stretched the open prairie, bisected by the stream, illuminated by the full moon. Willows bordered the stream, and would shield her from the prying eyes of cowboys. She pulled out her Colt and entered the willows, certain Indians wouldn't come this close. She couldn't take a bath with cowboys on guard, because she knew where their eyes would be.

As the drive progressed, they'd gotten worse, their eyes roving lecherously over her figure. If she saw one of them peeking at her while she was bathing, she'd shoot his whatchamacallits off.

One by one the cowboys meandered away from the campsite, and within minutes, it was deserted except for Ephraim. He sat on the wagon tongue and rolled a cigarette.

Sometimes Ephraim thought he was going to kill somebody. White people drove him crazy, and he couldn't fight back because lynchings, shootings, and nigra burnings took place fairly regularly. He had to be careful, and being careful meant acting stupid.

He thought of Cassandra, unapproachable, untouchable, attracted to John Stone. The heat rose to his face. He remembered the night in San Antone when he and Stone had confronted each other in an alley. It felt wonderful when his fist smashed Stone's face, but Stone shook it off as if it were the bite of a flea. The man had a head like rock, but Ephraim was sure he could defeat him. Pound the body, and the head would fall.

Ephraim lit the cigarette and threw the match into the fire. He puffed smoke and thought of how satisfying it would be to jump, with both boots, on John Stone's face.

Cassandra stepped out of her underwear and stood naked in the moonlight. A delicious fragrance arose from the stream, and she picked up the Colt and bar of bashed lavender soap.

The ground was moist beneath her feet, and she stepped gingerly on sticks and small rocks. The night breeze rolled over her stomach and blew through her hair, and the stream sang a bubbly tune. She spotted a boulder in the water, and decided that would be her base of operations. Her toe touched the stream, but it was colder than she'd expected. She waded toward the rock bravely, and shadows mottled the far side of the stream. Goose bumps broke out on her skin, and her feet were like ice. Shivering, she bent over and placed the Colt and bar of soap on the boulder.

The cowboys watched furtively behind trees and bushes on the other side of the stream. Their eyes were wide, their jaws hung open, and their heart rates increased considerably. They'd been lusting for her since San Antone, and there she stood naked in front of them, every man wishing he could put his hands on her. The bright moonlight revealed every nuance of her anatomy, and what they couldn't see, they imagined. They'd undressed her many times with their eyes, but she was lovelier than their wildest dreams.

Her breasts were perhaps a bit too large for a woman her size, but they weren't complaining. The ripe melons stood up proudly, her belly was smooth, and her fanny a perfect shape rare in nature. Stone was struck by how much she looked like Marie, and thought they must have kinfolk in common. But they weren't exactly identical. Marie had been slimmer and more delicate than Cassandra, and more poised. Marie also had a little of the devil in her, whereas Cassandra was serious and sensible, a typical rancher's wife, but her husband was dead and she was fair game.

She moved toward the center of the stream, and Stone was drawn to her succulent beauty. Marie probably was in bed with another man, doing all the wonderful things she'd done with him.

He couldn't forget her, and Cassandra brought her to mind whenever he looked at her, especially now. What'd happened to Marie? Was she dead or alive, or in a sanitorium, babbling about tea parties in the governor's mansion and dandelion wine.

Many nights he and Marie had gone swimming in streams at night like this. They'd sneak away from their homes and embrace in dark forests, with stars sparkling above and his heart beating wildly with joy, but it had been long ago, and all he had left was a broken photograph, a broken life, and memories that refused to die.

But now, out there in the stream, Cassandra Whiteside walked gracefully, naked as the day she was born. She was lovely, she liked him, and he was crouching in the bushes with a dozen other cowboys.

The cool current soothed her shapely limbs, and she wished she could bathe all night. She stretched her arms, dived beneath the silvery surface, and her breasts touched the smooth-pebbled depths.

She surfaced in the moonlight, and every cowboy stared at her with hopeless admiration and desire. Her skin looked like alabaster, as if formed by a master sculptor. She turned sideways to them, and rubbed soap into lather against her smooth flat belly.

Scrubbing hard, she systematically worked herself over, her skin tingling beneath her ministrations, while across the stream a group of men thought they were dying. Their throats were constricted, and they could barely breathe. If she told them to walk around on their tongues, they'd do it gladly.

She washed her breasts, and every cowboy was transfixed by the spectacle that lay before them, only twenty yards away. It pushed them over the line, and they gave rein to their most outrageously depraved fantasies. Every man held her in his arms as she luxuriated in the stream.

Stone's mouth was like gunpowder, and thought he'd go blind from his intense focus. A man needs his woman, otherwise he becomes a castrated steer.

Covered with suds, Cassandra dived beneath the black surface, and it rippled in widening halos to the shore. Stone shifted his vision and saw a figure creeping down the embankment, hatchet in hand.

It was an Indian, and the cowboys had been so quiet in their perversions, he hadn't even noticed they were there. He'd been scouting the area, heard Cassandra in the stream, come to investigate, and saw an opportunity to count coup.

Stone pulled out his Colt and took aim at the Indian creeping steathily toward Cassandra, the hatchet poised in his hand. Cassandra raised her head out of the water and heard footsteps rushing toward her. She turned around to a charging warrior!

The night exploded around Cassandra, and the warrior was ripped by lead before her eyes. An expression of shock came over his face, he stumbled, dropped his hatchet, and in his dying moments gazed at the cowboys rising up magically from the ground. He landed at Cassandra's feet, and she stared at him in horror as his blood trailed off in the stream.

Her cowboys advanced toward her, smoking guns in their hands. She ran to her clothing and draped it quickly over her wet skin as they crossed the stream. A ball of rage swelled in her craw when she realized they'd been there all the time, watching her like the degenerate individuals that they were. Then her attention was drawn back to the dead Indian, floating near the riverbank. Indians were bloodthirsty fiends, like coyotes and buzzards, and the only thing to do was kill them all.

"Spread out and see if there's any more of 'em!" Truscott hollered.

The cowboys entered the breaks on Cassandra's side of the stream, and Truscott marched toward Cassandra, who was shivering and trying to cover herself with the clothes in her hands. She was embarrassed to her toenails, and yelled: "What the hell're you doing here, Truscott!"

"Toldja there was injuns about, but you wouldn't listen! Din't think I know what I'm talkin' about! You wouldn't look so pretty right now, young lady, with that hatchet stickin' out of yer head!"

"Would you turn around, please?"

Cassandra dressed hastily, glancing toward the willows from which the Indian had come. She buttoned her shirt, while the cowboys and vaqueros returned with an Indian pony and guns in their hands.

"Must've been alone," said the *segundo*. "We plugged 'im good." Then he turned to Cassandra and gazed at her with bottomless depravity.

"If I ever catch you men peeping at me again, I'll shoot you where it hurts the most," she said. "Understand?"

The men shuffled their feet and wished they were somewhere else, embarrassed that she knew they'd been peeping at her, and she was even more embarrassed than they, because the only people in the world who'd ever seen her naked were her parents and mammy when she was small, and her husband.

She strapped the gun to her waist and tied the strap around her leg.

"Where'd you git the iron?" Truscott asked, noticing it for the first time.

"John Stone sold it to me."

Truscott spun around and faced Stone. "What you sell her a gun fer?"

"Protection."

"She's liable to shoot somebody by mistake."

"If I shoot somebody," Cassandra said levelly, "it won't be by mistake."

She picked up her dirty clothes and walked toward the campsite. The men watched her go, recalling her naked delicious body in the stream. No longer need they imagine what she looked like without clothes. They'd seen everything she had, and her most minute details had been committed to their turbid memories.

The *segundo* clicked his teeth. "If I ever get my hands on that filly, there won't be nothin' left when I'm finished."

"Take the injun's horse to the remuda," Truscott replied, "and double the guard on the herd."

Truscott pushed his hat to the back of his head and returned to the campsite. The cowboys followed, and the wrangler, Ben Thorpe, held the reins of the bareback Indian war pony. When they arrived, Cassandra was wondering where to put her tore-up blanket roll. She didn't want to be close to any of them, but they were her only protection.

She decided to sleep near the fire, and spread out her bedclothes beside it. The *segundo* walked toward her and held out his fist. Grinning, he let it open, and her underpants fell to her bedroll. "You forgot these, ma'am," he said with a wolfish grin.

"Thank you, Braswell."

Her face flushed crimson as she tucked the underpants into her gunny sack. Around her, the cowboys prepared for bed. She walked to the chuck wagon and said to Ephraim, "Got any more of that range coffee?"

He lifted the pot and poured some into a mug, and she carried it to the far side of the chuck wagon, facing north toward Abilene. She felt a presence nearby, and turned toward it. The *segundo* held a cigarette between his thick lips, and lit it. "Ma'am," he said in a hoarse whisper, "how'd you like to go off with me fer a leetle fun?" He lowered his eyes and stared frankly between her legs.

"Have you lost your mind?"

"I'll show you a real man, you go off with me." He cupped his groin with his hand. "I got what you need."

They heard a sound, and it was Ephraim rounding the front of the chuck wagon. Ephraim saw them together, and his eyes narrowed.

The *segundo* filled his lungs and hollered, "What the hell you lookin' at, burrhead! Git the hell out of here!"

Cassandra turned to the *segundo*. "This is his chuck wagon. You're the one who doesn't belong here."

Truscott appeared out of the darkness, craning his head. "What in tarnation is goin' on?"

The *segundo* turned to Cassandra. "I just asked you a question."

"Get away from me!"

He stared malevolently at her, then turned and walked to the front of the chuck wagon. "I'm hungry, goddammit! Cook me a steak, burrhead!"

"Finished all the meat," Ephraim replied. "Got to kill another steer."

"Then do it, you son of a bitch!"

Truscott stepped forward. "I give the orders around here. We'll kill another steer tomorrow. You've already had yer supper."

The *segundo* spun around and grabbed Ephraim by the front of his shirt. Ephraim was several inches taller than the *segundo*, but the *segundo* was wider, with massive biceps.

"This is yer fault, burrhead! Watch yer step or I'll put a hunk of lead in yer black ass!"

The *segundo* lifted Ephraim in the air, and Stone could see the torment on Ephraim's face.

"Sorry, boss," Ephraim said. "Din't mean no hurt."

"I'll put some hurt on you, boy, you ever talk back to me like that again."

"Let him down!" Cassandra shouted.

The *segundo* turned to her and sneered. "Is the nigra stickin' it to you, boss lady?"

Truscott stepped forward. "That'll be enough of that!"

The *segundo* threw Ephraim as if he were a toy, then faced Truscott. "You talkin' to me, old man?"

"You don't insult the boss lady unless you're ready to die." Truscott lowered his hand to his Remington, and looked ready to go the distance.

The *segundo* hesitated. He'd heard Truscott had been a gunfighter in his youth, and laughed. "You're gonna shoot me over that bitch? Why, you saw what she did to you tonight. She took off'n her clothes and practically did a hootchy-kootchy dance in the water. You think she din't know we was there? She's just another jezebel with fancy manners, but she don't kid me none. I ain't ready to die for the likes of her."

Cassandra whipped out her gun and pointed it at the *segundo*'s face. "You ever bother me again, I'll kill you."

The *segundo*'s face was pale as he stared down the barrel of her Colt.

"Get away from me," she said.

The *segundo* mumbled obscenities as he walked away, leaving Cassandra with the other cowboys beside the chuck wagon.

The ramrod drew himself to his full height. "I should've shot him."

"We need him," Cassandra said, "as long as he does his job. Now if you don't mind, gentlemen, I think I'll turn in."

She walked toward the campfire and lay on her blankets. A few seconds later Stone dropped his bedroll between her and the *segundo*, who was snuggling up with his mongrel dog.

The *segundo* hugged the dog and kissed his floppy flea-bitten ear, while the other cowboys threw their bedrolls around Cassandra, and she realized they wanted to protect her, or were they all like the *segundo*, waiting for the chance to get her alone.

She closed her eyes and tried to sleep as the fire diminished in the pit and the sounds of the night invaded the campsite.

Stone opened his eyes, awakened by his inner alarm clock. He knew it was time to ride night duty, although Don Emilio hadn't awakened him. Every extra moment of sleep counted, but as he was closing his eyes, he noticed something move at the edge of the campsite. Stone was about to sound the alarm, when the man stood, and moonlight shone on his face.

It was Ephraim, and Stone squinted in an effort to see what he was up to. Ephraim moved around the campsite silently as a big black panther, and then approached the *segundo*, who slept with his dog wrapped in his arms. Ephraim crouched near the *segundo*, picked up one of his boots, and poured something into it. Then he did the same with the *segundo*'s other boot. The sound of hoofbeats came to Stone's ears, and Ephraim disappeared into the night.

A few moments later Don Emilio rode into view. He climbed down from his horse and walked across the campsite, his spurs jangling in the night. When he reached Stone he stopped and said softly, *"Arriba."*

Stone opened his eyes slowly. "So soon?"

"Be glad it is not Sister Death, amigo."

Don Emilio returned his night horse to the remuda, and Stone crawled out from beneath his blanket. He sat on the ground and pulled on his boots, wondering what Ephraim had done to the *segundo*'s boots. He rolled his blanket and threw it into the chuck wagon, then looked at Ephraim lying in his blanket nearby. The incident was so strange Stone wondered if he'd dreamt it.

He walked to the remuda, feeling lopsided ever since he gave his gun to Cassandra. The horses were clustered in a rope corral, and Don Emilio removed the saddle from his night mount, throwing it onto the ground nearby.

"How're the cattle?" Stone asked.

"Sleeping like babies in their cribs. You have any tobacco left?"

Stone threw him his bag, and Don Emilio rolled a cigarette. "Tell me," Don Emilio said, "speaking as one caballero to another, do you think we should kill the *segundo*?"

"What for?"

"Sometimes, amigo, you are a stupid gringo, you know that? The hombre is *peligroso*—dangerous!"

"So am I, and so are you, but that's no reason to shoot a man."

"If we do not shoot him, he will shoot one of us."

"If you want to shoot him, go ahead. I don't give a damn either way."

"What do you think Truscott will say if I put a bullet in the *segundo*'s head?"

"He won't say a damn thing, as long as you do your job."

Don Emilio lit the cigarette, and Stone tightened the cinch under Tomahawk's belly. He let the stirrups fall, placed his foot in one of them, and raised himself smoothly into the saddle.

"It is so sad—about *La Señora*," Don Emilio said. "Here she is all alone without a man. I know you have seen a mare in heat—well, that is what *La Señora* will be for the next man. Do you think it will be you, amigo?"

"I think it'll be you, Don Emilio."

"It should be me, I agree completely, but she may choose you, because women are crazy."

"I'd say a man'd have to marry her, to sleep in her bed."

"What is wrong with that?" Don Emilio asked. "I have married far worse in my life, for far less." Don Emilio cocked an eye. "You know, I think you are in love with *La Señora,* but you do not even realize it yourself."

Stone didn't know what to say, so he touched a finger to his hat and spurred Tomahawk. The animal broke into a canter, and Stone headed toward the herd.

It was another clear starlit night on the prairie. Not one drop of rain had fallen since the drive began, and the longhorns were sleeping as Don Emilio had said. Stone heard a trumpet sound as an animal passed wind somewhere in the middle of the herd. A shooting star streaked across the heavens and disappeared behind buttes in the distance. Tomahawk plodded through the night, and Stone's mind wandered.

He thought of Cassandra standing naked in the moonlight, looking up at the sky. A mare in heat. Stone had seen mares tear up stables, nearly killing their studs and themselves.

He flashed on the Indian who'd attacked Cassandra, a beautiful ornate ceremonial war hatchet in his hand. Stone had been tempted to pick it up, but then Truscott ordered them to search the willows, and he'd forgotten. Maybe he could retrieve it on his way back to the camp, if nobody else got it. He could trade it for a bottle of whiskey in the first saloon they found, and maybe two bottles of whiskey if he talked fast enough. He made the firm decision to return to the stream for the hatchet when his two hours of night riding were finished.

• • •

The *segundo* gazed at the sleeping bodies around him. He'd just awakened, and figured it was a few hours before dawn. Raising his arm, he threw the blankets and his dog off him. Then he sat and pulled on his boots, and his feet slid in smoothly. He arose and looked around the campsite.

No one stirred, and he was tempted to shoot Truscott, but he'd have to fight the rest of the cowboys and didn't like the odds. Maybe someday, on a quiet range, he'd put a bullet through the back of Truscott's head, or maybe they'd meet in a cowtown someday, and he'd come up behind the old son of a bitch in an alley.

The *segundo* looked at Cassandra snuggled next to the fire. She'd spurned him, but the game wasn't over yet. It was a long way to Abilene, and he was sure she wanted him deep down. She'd just acted persnickety because the others were close by. Next time he'd git her alone, and show her what a man could do.

He made his way to the latrine, hearing the chorus of night birds and bugs. Tomorrow he'd kick the shit out of the burrhead, on general principles. The burrhead got uppity at times, and had to be put in his place.

He heard a rustle near the latrine and yanked out his gun. A large animal had brushed something, but maybe it was just the breeze and his sleepy mind playing tricks. Holstering his gun, he continued his stroll toward the latrine.

He became aware of how comfortable his boots were. He'd bought them new in San Antone shortly before he left, and they were broken in already, whereas you could wear some boots for ten years, and they wouldn't fit right. Finishing at the latrine, he returned to his blankets, and the boots felt so cool and nice he didn't bother to take them off. Dropping onto the ground, he pulled his blanket over his face and soon was snoring loudly.

Stone's nighttime guard duty was over, and he rode toward the campsite, thinking about whiskey.

The craving was on him, and he wiped his mouth with the back of his hand. If only he could have just one drink to warm his innards. But he had no whiskey, and there was no saloon nearby. Sooner or later they'd come to a town, and then maybe he could ride in. He had a few coins in his pocket, enough for a glass of whiskey.

The word "whiskey," came out of his mouth, and merely saying it evoked the dusky fluid. He imagined whiskey spilling over his tongue, trickling down his throat.

He'd spend the rest of his life in saloons, if he had unlimited wealth. But he detested saloons and wanted to live on the clear open range. He weighed the two wide-spaced irreconcilable desires as willows came into view. The stream was down there, with the Indian hatchet. He could hear the rush of water.

The deep blue night sky was pebbled with stars, and the willows alive with crickets. He was pooped out, and the drive had only just begun. If he were smart he'd return to the campsite immediately and turn in, but his mind was enchanted by the ornate tomahawk flashing through the air, not to mention the bottle of whiskey at the end of the rainbow.

The air became cooler as he approached the stream, and he heard its merry bubbling song. Ripples and wavelets were covered with the silver patina of moonglow, and he saw, lying in the shadows near the shore, the form of the dead Indian. Tomahawk was skitterish, dancing nervously to the side. Stone patted his mane and said, "I'll be right back, boy."

He climbed down from the saddle, adjusted his gunbelt, and walked toward the dead Indian. Stone's legs felt stiff; he'd be as bowlegged as Truscott by the time they got to Abilene. There was a pain in his back from constant riding, and he'd had a steady mild headache since leaving the ranch. A nauseating stench hit his nostrils, and he wondered if Slipchuck had taken a bath, his first in ten years.

He approached the Indian, whose form was dark and indistinct among the rushes at the edge of the stream. He recalled how the Indian had crept to Cassandra, to kill her. It was a good thing they were there to save her, but now she knew he'd been leering too, and it was embarrassing. Bending forward to look at the Indian more closely, his eyes widened with surprise when he saw the left shoulder and arm missing, while blood whorled in the water.

Something had been eating the Indian, and blood on the corpse was fresh, which meant the feeding had taken place recently. A low growl emitted from the dark willows, and Stone pulled out his gun. His scalp tingled as he peered into the shadows. What the hell was out there?

He heard a scrape and another growl. Stone ran toward Tomahawk, and a crashing massive hulk charged out of the willows. It was a black bear seven feet tall and nearly as wide, with arms big as tree trunks. Its mouth opened, and moonlight glinted on sharp white teeth.

"You leave me alone," Stone said in a low voice, "and I'll leave you alone." He understood now that it was not Slipchuck who'd been taking his first bath in ten years.

The bear snarled and advanced toward Stone, who was between him and his meal. Stone moved toward the woods, to get out of the bear's way, but the bear couldn't be placated so easily. Stone steadied his aim and fired. The bear roared and stared at Stone through tiny savage eyes as bullets shot into his tough hide.

Stone fired at the bear's head, and the night resounded with the explosions, but the bear kept coming, guttural sounds issuing from his throat. Stone fanned the hammer. Gunfire echoed across the plains. *Click.*

The gun was empty, and the bear only a few feet away. Stone pulled the Apache knife out of its sheath and rammed it into the bear's thick leathery belly. The bear wrapped his arms around Stone.

Stone's lungs compressed to nothing. Struggling for breath, all he got was flesh-besotted stench. He gulped wildly and stabbed the knife into the bear's eye. The bear screamed and reeled backward. Stone fell to the ground, while blood poured from the bear's eye.

Tomahawk attacked from the rear. The bear spun out and slammed Tomahawk alongside the head. Tomahawk fell to the ground, the stars spinning above him. *Remind me,* he thought, *never to fuck with bears again.* Stone pulled himself to his feet. Every bone in his chest felt broken. The bear swung a mighty paw, and Stone went flying through the air, landing in the water beside the dead Indian.

The taste of blood was in Stone's mouth, and kill was in the bear's heart. The hatchet glittered in the moonlight. Stone dived on it, rolled over, and came up with the weapon in his hand. The bear followed him, and Stone poised the heavy well-balanced implement of war, hearing the war drums of the Comanche nation pounding inside his skull. The bear swung a long-clawed paw at Stone, and Stone drove a hard chop into the bear's arm.

The bear let loose a shriek that tore the night apart, blood oozed from his wounds. Stone swung the hatchet with all his strength, and thought his arm had broken as he flew through the air, landing on his face in the mud. He rolled over, his left arm was covered with blood. The bear rushed toward him, snapping his teeth, got low and raked his claws across Stone's leg. Stone slammed the hatchet into the boulder that was the bear's head, and the blade of the hatchet tore a patch of fur off the creature's skull, but the force of the collision knocked Stone onto his back. The bear loomed above him, dripping blood onto Stone's face. Stone swung the hatchet at the bear's leg, and dove toward the woods, but he was slow, with broken bones, and blood soaking his torn shirt. The bear came after him, hopping on one leg, and whacked Stone from behind.

Stone was thrown onto his face, but rolled over quickly and swung the hatchet. The blade struck the bear's snout; he reared backward and howled. Stone picked himself off the ground and readied the hatchet, weak and woozy, nearly out on his feet. The curse was coming down hard—he saw the Gypsy fortune-teller's eyes in the eyes of the bear. The bear lumbered closer, his teeth dripping blood, and Stone said, "Come on, you son of a bitch! You want to fight—I'll give you a fight!"

The bear grabbed Stone, and Stone chopped. The bear fell on Stone, and ripped his claws across Stone's left shoulder, then back-slammed him in the face. Stone was hurled to the muck at the edge of the stream, and the bear bent over him, breathing heavily. A feeling of peace swept over Stone in the moment of ultimate surrender. *So this is it,* he thought. *Now I am the bear.* The bear bent over to dig his fangs into his kill.

Lightning struck him in fifteen places, a hideous surprise. He raised his arms and lumbered over the riverbank toward the cowboys on the riverbank, thunder spouting from their guns. He never faltered in his charge.

They ran out of his way, but one cowboy stood his ground in the middle of the path, holding double-barreled death in his hands. He was Duke Truscott, ramrod of the Triangle Spur, one eye closed, sighting down the barrels. "Come on you twisty old son of a whore!" Truscott hollered. "I'm a-ready for you!"

Truscott pulled both triggers. The bear stood headless in the path, blood gushing from his neck, and then collapsed onto his back. Smoke arose from the twin barrels of the shotgun, and Truscott licked his lips in satisfaction. The cowboys came out of the woods, guns in their hands.

"Nothin' better'n bear grease fer a man's boots," Truscott said.

Cassandra ran down the incline toward Stone, and saw him lying comatose, covered with blood. She kneeled beside him and felt his pulse.

"He's alive!"

He wasn't alive by much. His shirt was shredded and deep gashes oozed blood. He looked as if a butcher had gone to work on him. Cassandra knew they had to stop the bleeding, or else he'd drain dry. She untied her bandanna, dipped it in the water, and washed blood off Stone's face, but more welled from the lesions in his skin.

"Looks like a goner," Truscott said, ripping his own shirt for bandages. "Lost too much blood, I think."

Slipchuck kneeled on the other side of Stone, and reached for the hatchet, but even in the depths of unconsciousness, Stone refused to let his weapon go. He was carrying it with him to the ghost land of the Comanche nation, the bear dancing beside him.

4

THEY CARRIED HIM on a stretcher of blankets and lay him beside the burnt-out fire. Stone was dead weight, his blood seeped through the blanket and dripped to the ground.

Truscott wiped his nose with the back of his hand. "Git the shovel and dig the goddamned hole."

Slipchuck clasped his bony fingers around Stone's arm. "He'll pull through. God protects an honest cowboy."

"Bear sign all over the damn place, and this man walked right into it. I thought he was smart."

"He don't know spit about trackin'," Slipchuck said. "I'll teach 'im when he gets better."

"This man ain't gittin' better," Truscott said. "Goes to show you why we lost the war."

"Strongest man I ever met," Slipchuck said. "He'll be back."

Cassandra turned to Truscott. "Where can we find a doctor?"

"Nearest town I know is Colton, about five–six days north from here."

Joe Little Bear emerged from the woods, carrying his rifle.

"Where you been?" Truscott asked.

"Whenever white man hears shots, he runs toward them. Whenever Indian hears shots, he runs away from them." Joe Little Bear's eyes fell on Stone, lying by the fire.

"Damn fool picked a fight with a bear," Truscott said.

Slipchuck looked up at Joe Little Bear. "Know any good injun medicine?"

"The plants do not grow here." Joe Little Bear kneeled beside Stone and pulled back his eyelids. "This man will ride the ghost pony by dawn."

Slipchuck said, "The man ain't even daid yet, but already you're plannin' the funeral. I tell you, this is one strong son of a bitch. He was hit by a cannonball at Gettysburg."

Cassandra turned to Ephraim. "You'll have to make room for him in the chuck wagon."

Ephraim was looking toward the edge of the campsite, where a figure could be seen beneath blankets.

"Who's that?" Cassandra asked.

Truscott replied, "The *segundo* and his dog. Slept right through the whole mess. Ain't that a bitch?"

Cassandra touched Stone's hand, and it was cold as a corpse. She looked at his face, and the blood was coagulating. If he could stop bleeding, he'd have a chance. "The herd moves out on schedule in the morning, because the sooner we reach Colton, the better for John. Carry him to the chuck wagon, he'll be safer there."

Slipchuck said, "I know this man well enough to know he'd druther be in the open air, under the open sky. I'll look out for 'im."

The others left Slipchuck alone with Stone in the lee of the chuck wagon. The former stagecoach driver bent over his fallen pard and spoke softly, "We got lots of road ahead of us, Johnny. You're young, you ain't even seen half the whorehouses yet. Perfumed ladies with fancy underwears, the biggest tits you ever seen, covered with powder, lyin' on silk sheets, the best whiskey close to hand. We'll do it all, Johnny, you and me," the old man said, intoning his medicine chant.

Cassandra opened her eyes and saw the faint pale yellow glimmering of dawn on the horizon. The first thing she thought of was John Stone, and wondered if he'd survived the night.

She threw the blankets off and reached for her boot, carrying it closer. The triangular head of a rattlesnake reared out of the top, its forked tongue bidding her good morning. Cassandra screamed and jumped to her feet. Cowboys came up out of their blankets all around her, guns in hands. Don Emilio was closest, saw the rattler crawl out of Cassandra's boot, aimed his gun, and the rattler's head blew off.

"Señora," Don Emilio said with a slight bow, "always turn your boots upside down in the morning, because scorpions like them too, not to mention spiders and *las cucarachas*. Ah, but how could you blame them for wishing to be near your pretty little toes?"

Cassandra looked at the decapitated snake, then picked up the boot gingerly, to make sure nothing else had set up shop in it for the night. She sat on her blanket and pulled the boot on.

Slipchuck, Blakemore, and Duvall were gathered around Stone, and they made room for Cassandra. "He's still alive," Slipchuck said, eyes twinkling.

Cassandra knelt beside Stone's barely breathing body. Ephraim built a fire and placed his skillet on the grill as the men rolled their blankets. In the remuda, Tomahawk had a seven-inch gash on his neck. The *segundo*'s dog was whining pathetically, pushing his nose into the *segundo*, who still was fast asleep.

Truscott walked toward the *segundo* and said, "Time to get up, Braswell!"

The *segundo* didn't move. The mongrel cur got down on his stomach and pawed the ground, pathetic cries coming from his mouth.

"Braswell!" Truscott hollered.

The *segundo* was still, his head covered by his blanket. It was unhealthy to touch a sleeping cowboy, because he might wake up shooting, but Truscott kicked the *segundo*'s boot. "Let's hit it, Braswell!"

It was like kicking a dead man. Truscott bent over and rolled the *segundo* onto his back. The blanket fell away from the *segundo*'s face, and his complexion had turned purple; his eyes were closed, his mouth hung open, and his tongue was black. The dog let out a terrible shriek and jumped up, legs shivering.

"Looks like a goddamn turnip," Truscott said. "Must've drank horse piss."

The other cowboys gathered around. Truscott dropped to one knee and placed his ear against the *segundo*'s chest. He listened for several moments, then got to his feet, his brow wrinkled in mystification.

"This man's dead."

Everyone stared at the *segundo*. Only a few hours ago he'd been mean and cantankerous, and now he was dead? Slipchuck turned around, and saw Ephraim cooking steaks at the fire. Ephraim's eyes met his, and Slipchuck turned away quickly.

Truscott took off his hat and scratched his thinning sandy hair. "I'll be a hornswoggled son of a bitch."

Cassandra pushed through the crowd of cowboys. "What's wrong?" She looked down at the *segundo*, and her eyes widened.

"Dead," Truscott said, "but don't ask me how."

Cassandra was shocked. The *segundo* was even more hideous in death than in life. "Anybody know if he had family?"

"A drifter," Truscott said. "We'll bury 'im after breakfast."

They headed toward the campfire, and Ephraim threw steaks on their plates. Slipchuck didn't look at Ephraim as he passed the skillet, and the men sat on the ground, their backs to the dead *segundo*. The mongrel dog lay at the *segundo*'s feet, whimpering.

Cassandra dropped beside Truscott. "What usually happens to a man's belongings if he dies on the trail?"

"Cut a deck of cards, and the highest card takes his pick."

"I think I should have his rifle. I'm the only person here without one."

"You're the boss."

They finished breakfast, and the men took turns digging the *segundo*'s grave as the dog continued to mourn. Cassandra crawled into the chuck wagon and looked at John Stone. His lips were pale blue and only the slightest hint of breath escaped his nostrils. Cassandra took his hand and tried to rub life into it, but Stone was like a corpse. She'd escaped her creditors for the time being, but the cost was high.

Truscott's head appeared over the side of the chuck wagon. "We're ready to throw 'im in the ground. Care to say somethin'?"

Cassandra hitched up her gunbelt and walked across the campsite, her cowboy hat slanted low over her eyes. She came to a stop at the edge of the grave, and saw the *segundo* lying beside it, his boots still on, the dog licking his purple face.

The cowboys took off their hats and bowed their heads. Cassandra looked at the *segundo*. He'd been a dirty rotten son of a bitch. She couldn't say anything good about him.

"Dear Lord, please accept this man, Sylvester Braswell, into your loving care. He was a reliable cowboy. Ashes to ashes and dust to dust—the Lord giveth and the Lord taketh away." She looked at Truscott. He nodded to the cowboys, and they picked up the *segundo* by his hands and ankles, swung him over the hole, and let him go. He landed with a horrible crunch, and the vaquero Diego shoveled the earth on him as the dog stood at the edge of the grave and watched his master disappear beneath scoops of earth. Cassandra turned to the chuck wagon, and hoped she wouldn't have to do this for John Stone.

"Time to move out, ma'am."

The grave was a pile of stone with a cross in the middle. The dog lay at the foot of the grave and refused to leave. Cassandra placed her foot in the stirrup and lifted herself up.

They rode away from the grave, and Ephraim drove the chuck wagon, heading toward the herd. After fifty yards, they heard a terrible muffled scream behind them. They turned around in their saddles. The dog stared at the grave, his body trembling violently.

They heard the scream again, and it made Cassandra's blood curdle in her veins. She looked toward Truscott, and he peered at the grave, an expression of confusion and doubt on his face. Again the sound issued forth, a mournful wail that rent the vast stillness of the prairie, and the dog howled eerily, his nose pointed at the sky.

Truscott pulled his reins, but his horse whinnied and raised its front hooves in the air, refusing to go toward the grave. Truscott put the spurs to him again, and the horse still wouldn't move forward.

The other horses were likewise spooked, their ears pointed straight up and whining sounds erupting from their throats. Truscott jumped to the ground and advanced staunchly toward the grave, gun in hand. "Git the shovel!"

A hoarse shriek emanated from the grave, and everybody stopped in their tracks. The rocks were undulating, as if the *segundo* were trying to fight his way out of the ground. The dog danced about crazily, howling and barking, snapping his teeth at the air. Cowboys threw the rocks off the grave, then dropped to their hands and knees and clawed at the dirt.

Moans and yelps came from the earth buckling and churning beneath their hands. An agonized screech arose from the ground, followed by an explosion of dirt into the air. A hand appeared out of the grave, and a second later a head covered with dirt could be seen.

The *segundo* sat up in his grave. Slowly he raised his head, his eyes opened, and a strange nasal snort came out of his mouth. The dog trembled, eyes bugging out of his head. Everybody stepped back. The *segundo* snorted and leaned from side to side as his unblinking eyes roved the circle of cowboys and vaqueros around him. He stared blankly at Ephraim for a few moments, then pressed his hands against the ground and raised himself up.

The *segundo* was covered with dirt, his face had no life, and flesh hung loosely on his bones. "Unnh," he said, and turned slowly toward Truscott. "Unnh."

The dog looked at the *segundo*, a terrible choking sound erupting from the dog's mouth. Then, with a fearful wail, the dog turned and ran away from the campsite. The cowboys stared at the terrified creature as it disappeared into the endless wastes of Texas.

Truscott gazed mystified at the spot where the dog had gone, then turned to the *segundo*, standing stiffly, covered with dirt. Truscott had seen a white buffalo once a long time ago, but never anything like this.

"Wrangler, get this man a horse!"

They didn't know if the *segundo* were alive, dead, or somewhere in between. Slipchuck glanced at Ephraim, and Ephraim's face was a block of cold ebony. The *segundo*'s chest heaved as he sucked in large quantities of fresh prairie air, and his arms hung loosely down his sides. Cassandra couldn't tear her eyes from him. He'd risen from the grave like a monster or a ghost, but his old swaggering self was gone. This was a meek hulking creature with no will of his own.

Truscott cleared his throat. "Braswell—from now on you'll ride the drag."

"Unnh."

The wrangler returned with an extra horse, climbed down from his saddle, and led the extra horse to the *segundo*, who stepped forward woodenly and took the reins. The *segundo* raised himself jerkily into the saddle, and sat hatless in the sun, staring at the horizon.

"Vacation's over," Truscott growled to him. "Git to work."

● ● ●

An hour later the herd was moving north again, a dead man riding the drag, and before them stretched endless plains, mesas, and valleys, with thin transparent clouds scudding across the blue sky.

But the sky didn't look so blue on the drag, where clouds of dust kicked up by thousands of hooves billowed about the riders, obscuring their vision.

Cassandra sat on her horse, breathing through the red bandanna over her mouth and nose, watching cows and steers. They were the same ones every day, and each had his or her special quirks, as Cassandra and her horse rode back and forth behind them, forcing laggards to stay with the others.

Occasionally the *segundo* would appear out of the rolling clouds of dust, riding his horse. He sat loosely in his saddle, was covered with dirt, and seemed more beast than man. Cassandra shuddered whenever she saw him.

Stone was returning from Comanche ghost land, floating through a vast cold sea of darkness. He didn't know who or where he was, where he'd been, or where he was going. He was just a faint glimmer of consciousness in the infinity of time.

Sometimes he lost what little consciousness he had, and there'd be endless nothingness. The chuck wagon rolled over the prairie, and he rocked from side to side amid the skillet, grill, stewpot, and other utensils of the culinary arts, as the spirit of a raging bear growled over him.

Ephraim sat on the high seat, the reins in his hands, and looked back at Stone periodically, but Stone was always the same, lifeless and pale, covered with ridges of dry blood. Ephraim had been one of the first to arrive at the stream the previous night, and seen the bear deliver the final wallop that sent Stone flying.

It was a blow that would've killed most other men, and Ephraim remembered their clash in San Antone, when he'd hit Stone with his best punches, and Stone'd kept fighting. Now he had Stone at his mercy, but it'd give him no pleasure to simply slit Stone's throat. He wanted to *defeat* him in toe-to-toe combat, so Stone would know who was the better man.

Stone groaned softly, and Ephraim turned around. "You'll pull through," Ephraim said through clenched teeth, "and then you'll be mine."

A wave of unbearable agony swept over Stone, and all he could do was moan deep in his throat. He was roasting alive, his skin crackling, bones melting, guts bursting. He wanted to escape, but couldn't get away. The suffering was all-engulfing, like a sea of torment that dropped on a man and never washed away.

Occasionally it became too intense, and he fainted from its incessant pressure. He had no will, no concept, only blackness, but then the pain would draw him to dim awareness again, and he'd wallow in it, unable to rise.

He alternated between total blackout and faint consciousness for the rest of the day, and at night, after the herd had bedded down, the cowboys carried him out of the chuck wagon and lay him in the open air. Cassandra knelt beside him and gazed at his waxen features. She touched her sweaty palm to his forehead, and it was like a furnace.

"That's good," Truscott said. "Kill the infection. Listen, you and me gotta have a talk."

Cassandra followed Truscott into the darkness on the other side of the chuck wagon. "I can't run this spread by myself," he said. "We need a new *segundo*. Usually, the way it works is I make my recommendations to the boss, and the boss makes the decision, you want to work it that way?"

"Who do you recommend?"

"Either Maldonado or Luke Duvall. Offhand I'd say Duvall, because he's a white man, but Maldonado owned his own ranch down by the Nueces, and prob'ly knows cattle better."

"If Maldonado knows cattle better, he gets the job."

"Should I tell 'im, or do you want to?"

"I'll tell him."

She washed her hands and face in the basin, dried herself with the dirty communal towel, and saw Don Emilio approach from the direction of the campfire. Flames aureoled behind his stocky figure, and he had a black mustache over flashing white teeth.

"You wanted to see me, señora?"

"I've spoken with the ramrod, and we want you to take Braswell's job. Pays ten dollars more a month. Report to Truscott, and he'll tell you what to do."

"I know what to do, señora. I have owned more cattle than you ever dreamed of."

Cassandra looked at him, and he projected fierce masculine pride. His hair was thick and straight, parted to the side, and three buttons of his shirt were undone, showing his powerful chest. A confident expression was on his face, and his eyes were pulling down her jeans.

"We need your experience, Don Emilio. We still have a long way to go before Abilene."

"I am your slave, señora."

Cassandra awakened as the first ray of dawn peeked over the rolling hills to the east of the campsite. She gingerly lifted her boots and slapped them a few times to get rid of possible deadly creatures. Then she walked toward the chuck wagon, where Stone lay on the ground.

He still was out; she touched her hand to his brow. It was like a rock in the hot sun, and he looked slimmer, as if his musculature were burning up in the heat. It'd be a terrific loss if he died, he was so young, and went through five years of war only to be killed in a mindless encounter with a bear. Between the Indians and wild animals, there was no time to be as lackadaisical as Stone must've been when he'd walked into the bear. It was a lesson he'd never forget, if he lived to learn it. The next twenty-four hours would tell the story.

Cassandra and the men ate their usual breakfast of fried steaks, and were on the trail at five o'clock in the morning. A thick layer of gray clouds covered the sky, and it looked like rain. The first drops fell at ten, and by noon the trail had become a sea of mud.

No longer was there a cloud of dust on the drag, and the cattle slowed to a crawl. One old bull sat and refused to move, and Cassandra climbed down from her saddle, took her coiled lasso in hand, and beat his rump, but he wouldn't budge.

The *segundo* rode toward her on his horse, and looked down at the bull. He hadn't bathed since coming out of the ground, and dirt on his body was streaked by rain. He jumped to the ground, worked his arms under the bull's body, and lifted the bull off the mud, an act of inhuman strength. Then he kicked the bull viciously, and the bull bellowed, running back to the drag.

Cassandra watched the *segundo* walk stiffly to his horse and climb aboard. He rode away, to search for the next recalcitrant animal, and Cassandra scratched her head. He wasn't living and he wasn't dead, but he was the best cowboy she had. She remounted her horse and hit the spurs. The horse plodded through the rain, and Cassandra could hear drops of water falling on the hood of her oilskin poncho.

The rain diminished in late afternoon, and in the evening they camped beside another stream. Truscott had shot an antelope earlier in the day, and Ephraim fried antelope steaks. They ate around the campfire, too tired to speak.

Cassandra was filthy and sweaty, and wanted to bathe in the stream, but didn't know how to do it. Somehow she had to figure out a way to wash safely, without cowboys ogling her. They couldn't be trusted, and probably laughed among themselves at her predicament. They only respected loaded guns pointed at their faces, so that's what she'd give them.

She finished supper, and found the carcass of the antelope. Ephraim had cut off the creature's head, and it lay in the grass on the far side of the chuck wagon, where lobos stared at it from behind a prickly pear cactus, but Cassandra didn't know they were there. She picked up the gory head and carried it to a boulder four feet high at the edge of the campsite, where all could see it.

Then she returned to the campfire, faced them, and said, "I'm going to take a bath, and I'll need four guards. Do I have any volunteers?"

Every man, except Ephraim, raised his hand.

Cassandra picked Slipchuck, Blakemore, Diego, and Pedro, and they rose to their feet, smiling happily at the prospects that lay ahead.

"Two of you'll be on the far side of the stream," she said, dropping her voice into the lower registers, "and two on the near side. Your backs will be to me at all times, because you're supposed to be watching for Indians, bears, and whatever in hell else might be out there. If I see any man looking at me, this is what'll happen to him."

She pulled her gun, raised the barrel, and took aim at the antelope's skull. Her tongue sticking out the corner of her mouth, she pulled the trigger. Her gun flashed, the report echoed, and the antelope's head split like a rotten watermelon.

Cassandra blew smoke from the end of her gun barrel. "If you don't think you can handle the job, say so now."

Nobody spoke.

"Let's get it over with," she told them, dropping her gun into its holster.

She picked up her towel, shredded by two stampedes, and headed toward the stream, followed by her four guards, who, though they'd promised not to look, managed to take quick glances out of the corners of their eyes as she bathed, and they expected a bullet at any moment. But not even the promise of lead could stop an honest cowboy.

Stone looked worse in the morning. His breathing was practically nonexistent and he was still as a corpse. *He's going to die,* she thought. *No doubt about it.*

Cassandra bent over and kissed his hot forehead, and the odor of death clung to his dark blond hair. She ran her fingers through it, and came upon a big scab.

"Keep a close eye on him," she said to Ephraim. "He looks awful bad."

"Leave him to me," Ephraim said.

Cassandra walked back to her horse and raised herself into the saddle. She wheeled her horse and rode to Truscott's side at the head of the cowboy crew returning to the herd.

"How far you think we are from that town?" Cassandra asked.

"Maybe two days."

"I don't think John Stone'll make it."

"Never been on a drive where somebody din't git killed."

Cassandra could hear the chuck wagon bouncing and creaking over the uneven terrain. In New Orleans there'd been hundreds of doctors, and even San Antone had several. Never had she been in a situation where there was no doctor within a reasonable distance. On the prairie nothing seemed within reach, except death.

They approached the edge of the herd, and Diego was guarding a cow who'd given birth to a calf during the night. *How beautiful,* Cassandra thought as she rode closer. The calf was dark brown like its mother, standing on spindly legs, sucking its mother's teat.

"I'll take care of it," Truscott said, lowering himself to the ground. "Git that cow back to the herd."

Truscott grabbed the calf and pulled it away from its mother. The calf bawled in surprise, and its mother mooed angrily. Diego rode his horse toward the mother and whapped her in the face with his lasso. Another cowboy slapped her haunch. The mother tried to join her crying calf, but the cowboys beat her off and pushed her toward the herd. Truscott advanced toward the calf and pulled his six-gun.

"What're you going to do?" Cassandra asked.

"Shoot 'im," Truscott said matter-of-factly, aiming his gun at the quivering newborn creature.

Cassandra jumped down from her horse and ran toward him, and he turned, his brow wrinkled with confusion.

"What the hell's botherin' you *this* time?"

"You're not going to kill that calf, Truscott!"

"We can't take it with us, because it'll slow down the herd, and if I don't kill it, the coyotes will. How'd you rather die, Mrs. Boss Lady—a quick bullet in the head or get torn apart by coyotes?"

He raised his gun and drew a bead on the bleating calf, while in the distance the cries of its mother could be heard. Cassandra rushed forward and grabbed Truscott's wrist. The gun fired, exploding a patch of dirt beside the calf.

Truscott turned to Cassandra, and his eyes were popping out of his head. "I knowed the first day I seen you I should've walked the other way! You don't know nothin', and you're always in my goddamn road!"

His face red with rage, he threw his hat vehemently to the ground. Cassandra knelt beside the calf and wrapped her arms around its neck. It was a baby, trembling against her body. Truscott picked up his hat, whacked it against his knee, and pulled it on his head.

"You got three choices," he said. "We can stop the herd until this calf can travel, prob'ly two to three weeks. You can leave the mother with the calf, and the coyotes'll git 'em both. Or you can shoot the goddamn calf. When you make up yer so-called mind, tell me what you want." He walked to his horse and climbed into the saddle. "What the hell're you men lookin' at! You got a job to do—so git ridin'!"

Cassandra hugged the frightened calf as the cowboys whooped and hollered, getting the herd into motion. The cattle protested noisily, and the pitiful cries of the mother still could be heard.

"Now, now," she said to the calf, trying to comfort it. If she hadn't interfered with Truscott, the calf would be dead and the issue over and done with. She grit her teeth in frustration, while the calf tried feebly to join its mother. It was still damp with birthing fluids. *I can't kill it,* she thought.

She pinched her lips together and drew her Colt. The calf gazed at her with big innocent eyes, and she aimed at its head, grit her teeth, and pulled the trigger. The explosion echoed across the prairie, and the calf's head was blown apart, blood and brains all over the grass. Cassandra felt light-headed and numb as she rose to her feet. *God forgive me.*

"Water . . ." Stone's eyes were half-opened, and he saw blurry light as sun baked the torn canvas roof of the chuck wagon. The road rolled him from side to side, and every movement caused sharp suffering at numerous points of his anatomy. He was in a world of violent raging pain, unable to rise into full consciousness.

"Water . . ."

He was vaguely aware of who he was, that he'd been hurt, and might die. A great weight was dragging him deeper into a black pool, and he struggled to climb out. The endless oblivion frightened him, and somehow he had to stay alive. He focused on the chuck wagon roof, and told himself as long as he could see it, he'd live.

"Water . . ." His throat was dry, his tongue was swollen, and his guts felt like cardboard. He thought he might live, if he could get a little water. Just a few drops. Then a dark form appeared above him, and a familiar voice said, "How's it goin', Massa John?"

Stone knew who it was, and a chill went up his back. He was helpless, and his enemy could skin and bone him alive. "Water . . ." he croaked.

Ephraim held up his canteen. "This what you want, Massa John? Well, let me tell you, I knows how you feels. I felt the same way many times, workin' in your daddy's fields, pickin' your fuckin' goddamned shit-cotton!"

Stone was barely conscious, and his mind functioned only at its most rudimentary level, but he knew he wasn't getting any water. He gathered together his remaining reserves of strength and said, "You son of a bitch!"

"I might be the son of yer daddy, for all you know, Massa John—ever think 'bout that? And don't go tellin' me it couldn't be, 'cuzz you knows your daddy come to the slave quarters at night. Lots of his chillun was workin' in the fields, and I might've been one of them, you never can say for sure. Stranger thangs have happened in Beulah Land."

Stone was at Ephraim's mercy, and there was nothing he could say. He struggled to breathe, as a great weight pressed on his chest.

"You know, Massa John—a slave can't have a drink whenever he wants, like a white man, becuzz while the slave is drankin', he ain't pickin' none of your daddy's cotton. About every two–three hours we could drink, so maybe I should make you wait that long, to know what it's like."

Stone wished he could punch Ephraim in the mouth, but couldn't budge. Ephraim looked at Stone contemptuously, then leaned forward and grabbed the front of Stone's ragged shirt, bringing his face close to Stone's.

"I don't want you to die, Massa John. It be too good for you. I want to kill you with my own two hands, and you fall at my feet, and kick your fuckin' white face!" Ephraim held out the canteen. "I gonna keep you alive, because your ass belongs to me!"

Ephraim raised Stone's head, and touched the canteen to his lips. Stone felt the water trickle over his tongue, and it was ambrosia. He struggled to swallow it through a mangled torn throat.

" 'At's enough for now, Massa John. You don't wanna drank too much the fust time." Ephraim pulled the canteen from Stone's mouth and screwed the cap on. "I never thought I'd see the day I'd take care of you, but I'm lookin' down the road to when you're well . . . if you git well. You might git the pizzoned blood and rot real slowlike, and stink like shit. I guess if that happens, Truscott'll put you out of your misery. We'll bury you and I'll come back at night and piss on your grave."

Ephraim disappeared, and Stone felt the wagon rocking from side to side again. He closed his eyes and thought of being buried on the prairie, and Ephraim coming back at night to piss on him, but maybe it wouldn't matter, if a man was already dead.

Stone thought of Ephraim, and felt his fighting spirit return. He wanted to kill the ex-slave, and that gave him something to live for. Then he lost sense of himself, sinking into the dark night, as the old beat-up chuck wagon rolled across the plains.

Stone was awakened by Marie's voice. He opened his eyes to half mast and saw her face floating above him. A flood of joy passed through his body, obliterating the pain for a few moments, and he struggled to raise his arms.

"Marie . . ."

"He doesn't know where he is," Cassandra said. She sat with Stone's head on her lap, and the cowboys gathered around. His color was better.

Ephraim handed a bowl of beef broth to Cassandra. "John," she said, "you've got to eat something."

Stone struggled to open his mouth. She touched the spoon to his lips, and warm meaty flavor rolled over his tongue. He swallowed laboriously, and saw Marie smile.

"Very good, John. Now let's try it again, all right?"

Slipchuck knelt beside her. "I heerd it said, the best thing fer a man at the end of his rope is . . ." The old stagecoach driver removed his hat and looked at her sincerely as he searched for the appropriate word. "I don't want to stomp on yer boot, or say somethin' a man shouldn't in front of a woman,'specially if the woman's his boss lady, but Johnny's like a son to me, and I'd say what he needs most right now is a mouthful of good titty."

Her face registered horror, then astonishment, and finally compassion, as she realized the old wreckage was doing his best to help, and had just pulled one out of the hopelessly twisted memories of a million nights alone. "I'd do anything for my men, Slipchuck, but I don't think that's an accepted medical practice."

"Mebbe not," Slipchuck said, "but it works anyways. I remember once on a run to Denver fer the old Pitkin Line, we was attacked by injuns, and I got an arrow right through me chest." Slipchuck pulled open his shirt, and proudly showed the scar on his bony chest that sprouted a few scraggly gray hairs. "Everybody thought I was a dead duck, and I bled like a stuck pig, but we had a young lady fer a passenger, and she gimme some of her titty, and I'm alive today."

"She did this voluntarily, or was she forced?" Cassandra asked, trying to imagine herself in such an outlandish situation.

"Wa'al, it was like this. She was on her way to the best cathouse in Denver, but she cut her ordinary price in half, bein' as we was all in the same mess together."

The nighthawk traveled miles without seeing anything unusual, and then suddenly up out of the night, in the midst of a vast wilderness, were the dying embers of a fire, a chuck wagon, and dark forms lying on the ground in blankets.

The nighthawk continued his journey, and John Stone saw him silhouetted for a brief moment, against the moon. The breeze blew a lone tumbleweed across the campsite, through the fire pit, bouncing and spinning west toward the Pecos. He felt weak as a newborn babe, and couldn't even raise his head off the pillow Cassandra had made out of her rolled clothing. She slept on her side a few feet away, her lovely profile aglow with moonlight.

Stone saw Slipchuck, Duvall, Calvin Blakemore, and Don Emilio Maldonado sleeping around him. He remembered the bear's long white fangs and big paws tipped with blood. When the beast struck him, he'd thought his whole body was coming apart. He'd fought Yankee soldiers and savage Indians at close quarters, but the bear had been a new dimension in hand-to-hand combat, and he'd never forget the stench.

Cassandra rolled onto her back, and he could see the outline of her breasts against her cowboy shirt. She'd fed him broth, as if he were a baby and she his mother. He looked at the mountains in the distance, and saw faces in their shadow formations. They looked like old men, and they said to him: *We will be here long after you are gone, but one day we will not be here either.*

The last thing he saw was Cassandra's profile in the moonglow.

The next morning the cowboys propped Stone against the wheel of the chuck wagon, and he ate stew made from beef chunks and beef blood, his hand shaking every time he raised the spoon to his mouth.

Cassandra and the cowboys ate steaks, and Stone was surprised by the change that'd come over the *segundo*. He was filthy, his movements suggested a mechanical doll, and his complexion was the strangest shade of purple. Stone turned to Cassandra and said weakly, "What happened to him?"

Cassandra told the story from when they'd found the *segundo* dead, the funeral, and the resurrection of the *segundo* out of his grave. "Strangest thing I've ever seen in my life," Cassandra said. "Evidently it affected his brain."

Stone stared at the *segundo*. He'd been the most brutal cowboy in the bunch, and now was subdued. "When'd you find him dead?"

"The morning after you fought the bear."

Stone remembered Ephraim fooling with Braswell's boots that night, and looked at Ephraim, sitting cross-legged on the ground, slicing his steak with fork and butcher knife. What had Ephraim done to the *segundo*'s boots?

They cleaned their plates, broke camp, and placed Stone in the chuck wagon, propping him against the slats so he could see the mountains. Stone rolled a cigarette, spilling half the tobacco onto his lap, as a wheel hit a prairie dog hole. Ephraim sat sturdily on the seat, the reins wrapped around his big hands. Stone scratched a match against the floor of the wagon and lit the cigarette.

Stone was weak, and the cigarette hung loosely at the corner of his mouth as he turned to Ephraim and said in a barely audible voice, "What you put into the *segundo*'s boots, Ephraim?"

Ephraim spun his head around. "What you talkin' 'bout!"

"I saw you spill something into the *segundo*'s boots the night before he died. What in hell've you done to him?"

Ephraim regained his composure and grinned. "Nothin' compared to what I'm a-gonna do to you, Massa John. I'm a-gonna rip your heart out, you sickly white shit, and use it for stew meat."

"I won't be sickly long."

"I could cure you like *that*"—Ephraim snapped his fingers—"but I wants you to suffer. Darkies're s'posed to be dumb, but I ain't never heard of no darky walkin' onto a bear." Ephraim tied the reins to the brake lever, climbed in back with Stone, pulled his knife, and touched the blade to Stone's throat. "If you knew how much I hated you, you'd shake in your boots. I could take your head off right now, and that be the end of you." Ephraim's lips trembled, and his eyes bulged out of his head. "I'll take care of you later," he said.

Stone was a few shades paler as he inhaled the cigarette. There was something unnerving about a blade held to the throat. He had no strength, was totally vulnerable, even a child could kill him.

It reminded him of Gettysburg, where he'd stopped a chunk of grapeshot. It went in beneath his ribs on the left side, and blew him out of his saddle. He lay on the ground as fighting raged all around him, but fortunately the Yankees had too many healthy Johnny Rebs to contend with, and Stone had survived.

But if Indians attacked, he couldn't fight. He was at everybody's mercy, and Ephraim could humiliate him at will. If I ever get out of this alive, I'll rip his head off and feed it to the buzzards.

That evening at the campfire Stone chewed steak and boiled roots Ephraim had gathered earlier near a water hole. He didn't have much strength in his jaws, but managed to get it down.

He took a few steps after supper, then his knees buckled and he was caught by Blakemore and Duvall, who'd been standing on either side of him, waiting for him to fall. They propped him against a wheel of the chuck wagon, and Truscott approached with Cassandra.

"Think you can ride tomorrow?" Truscott asked Stone.

"If I had to."

"Colton's a few hours ride from here, and they got a sawbones. I'm sendin' men fer supplies, and you can go with 'em, but it's up to you. Hard ridin' might open yer wounds, and you'll ride hard if you run into injuns."

"I'll try."

"We'll git yer horse ready in the mornin'."

Truscott walked away, and Slipchuck sat beside Stone, placing his hand on Stone's shoulder. "Now that you're gittin' better, Johnny, I got to tell you that was a damn fool thing you did with that bear. His tracks was all over, his stink was like a shit fog, but that din't make no difference to you. You got to look where you're goin', boy. When you're strong, I'm a-gonna be yer teacher, and after I'm done, you'll read sign like an injun, but sometimes I think you ain't got a damn thing between yer ears 'cept dead flies—the damn dumb things you do. Enuff to make a man wonder how you got this far in life without gittin' a bullet up yer ass, or endin' up supper in some animal's gut."

Slipchuck's gaze returned to the fire. It wasn't the first time he'd sat beside a beat-up pard. The queer thing about men, the old stagecoach driver reflected, is that they keep on a-comin'. And if Cassandra had given John Stone a little of her sweet titty, he'd already be a-dancin' the Houlihan.

5

IN THE MORNING, Stone felt the beef blood in his veins. His hand didn't shake as much as he held the spoon for breakfast. He placed tender cuts of beef into his mouth, thinking about what Slipchuck had said last night.

He'd blundered onto the most dangerous animal on the prairie, because he'd been dreaming of booze, the curse of his life. A man's fate hung on the thread of his concentration, and everybody knew what liquor did to concentration.

He heard a shout on the other side of the campfire, and two vaqueros jumped to their feet, hollering at each other. A crowd gathered around them, and then the two stepped back and drew long knives. Don Emilio walked between them and spoke in rapid-fire Spanish. They shouted back, a cacophony of voices, and tried to work around Don Emilio, so they could slash each other. One vaquero was Roberto, short and squat, with long hair to his shoulders and the face of a pig. The other was Manuelo, with a thin drooping mustache like a rat's tail over his upper lip.

Stone couldn't speak Spanish, but knew terrible insults were going down. Both men strained to reach each other, their knives gleaming in the dawn light. *A hell of a thing to wake up to,* thought Stone. Don Emilio's voice was soft, reasoning, pleading. Finally, after much haranguing, the two adversaries nodded to each other as if they'd made an agreement.

Don Emilio turned to Truscott and said, "I am afraid this

matter will have to be settled in blood."

"Git it over with," Truscott replied. "We got a herd to move."

Don Emilio talked to the combatants, and they sheathed their knives. Turning contemptuously from each other, they walked toward their horses.

Cassandra looked at Truscott. "Would you mind telling me what's going on?"

"Them two greasers is gonna fight it out."

"Fight *what* out?"

Truscott shrugged. "Only come onto it at the end, and I heerd one of 'em say something' 'bout *camisa roja*."

"What's that?"

" 'Red shirt' in greaser talk."

"You mean they're fighting over a shirt?"

" 'Pears so."

"Don't you think you should try to stop them?"

"You don't stop two men when they want to kill each other."

"*Kill* each other? I can't afford to lose any cowboys, you thick-skulled son of a bitch!" Cassandra ran toward the two vaqueros. "Wait a minute!"

Don Emilio stepped in front of her, and she tried to move around him, but he blocked her way. "It is a matter of honor," he said. "You must leave them alone."

Cassandra narrowed her eyes at him. "I'm ordering you to stop them, and don't tell me you can't do it, because I know you can. You brought them with you from the brush country, and they do whatever you say."

"Señora, you do not understand. These men live by a code, and when there is an insult, someone must die. There is no other possibility."

"Out of my way!" She tried to walk through Don Emilio, but he held her wrists.

"Do not interfere," he said. "This is not woman's business."

"This herd is my business, and I can't afford to lose men! If they want to die for a shirt, they can do it when we get to Abilene!"

"I am afraid it is too late for that, señora."

"Let me go!" She struggled to break away from his grip, but his hands were steel clamps on her wrists. "Truscott, do something!"

"Can't do nothin' till one of them greasers kills each other, and you're holdin' up the show. Can't you ever keep yer mouth shut, woman?"

Cassandra was so angry she could spit. She pitched and tossed, trying to break Don Emilio's grip, and he laughed, his white teeth flashing. She tried to butt him with her head, and he whirled like a matador, ending up behind her, his body touching hers, and he still held her wrists tightly.

"You are a wild thing," he whispered into her ear, "but I am the man who can tame you."

A strange thrill passed up her spine, while the two vaqueros mounted their horses. She yelled: "Stop it!"

They ignored her, turned their horses around, and rode away from each other. Cassandra tried to break loose, but Don Emilio held her snugly against him. She could feel the strength of his body, and knew she could never break his iron grip.

The vaqueros rode until they were two hundred yards apart, then turned and faced each other. They took their lassos in hand, made loops, and twirled them over their heads in ever-widening arcs. Then they spurred their horses, and the horses galloped toward each other, gathering speed while the vaqueros swung ropes over their heads. When they drew close, they threw their lassos at each other. Both missed, and they rode past each other, gathering up the ropes.

Cassandra turned toward Don Emilio. "What're they trying to do?"

"You will see soon enough, señora."

She brought her heel down hard on his foot, and he yelped, letting her go. She ran toward the two vaqueros and held out her hands for them to stop, but they kept galloping onward, swinging lassos gracefully over their heads.

"That's enough!" she yelled. "I'll buy you all the goddamned shirts you want!"

The ground shook beneath her feet as the horses bore down on her. She jumped back, and Roberto thundered past, hurling his lasso at Manuelo, who at the same moment tried to rope Roberto.

Roberto's lasso knocked off Manuelo's sombrero, and Manuelo's lasso didn't even come close. They continued riding and winding in their lassos, to prepare for another run. A hand wrapped itself around Cassandra's forearm. She thought it was Don Emilio again, and turned to give him a piece of her mind when she saw Slipchuck, a troubled expression on his face.

"You best step back, ma'am. This ain't no place to be a-standin'. If two men're gonna kill each other, you might as well let 'em git on with it."

The two vaqueros charged again, heads down, lassos dancing in the air. Cassandra stared at them, wondering what was wrong with men that made them do these things. Strings of froth flew from their horses' mouths as they closed the gap, and the two vaqueros were bent forward in their saddles, leaning toward each other, whirling the big loops through the air. When they were twenty yards apart they let fly.

Roberto's lasso dropped like a halo around Manuelo. An expression of panic came over Manuelo's face, and a mad smile creased Roberto's porcine features. He pulled the rope hard, spurred his horse, and Manuelo flew out of his saddle. *Santa Maria*, thought Manuelo as he fell to the ground. *Pray for me at the hour of my death.*

Cassandra watched in horror as Manuelo hit the grass, bounced, and was dragged away at top speed by Roberto. Manuelo screamed in pain as he slammed into rocks and bushes, turning red as he was flayed alive.

Roberto looked backward in his saddle, at his fallen adversary. He could stop his horse and let Manuelo up, but it would defile Manuelo's honor. *He must die,* thought Roberto, all anger gone, and a tear in his heart for his fallen *compañero*, but so it must be. *I will wear that red shirt,* amigo *to the end of my days.*

Cassandra closed her eyes, but could hear Manuelo crashing through thorns and prickly pear, screaming horribly. She thought she'd go mad for a few moments, but the sounds diminished as Roberto rode farther away. She opened her eyes and saw Don Emilio in front of her.

"I could never respect a man who'd let something like that happen," she said to him.

"You are a silly woman, and you know nothing of men, but you are very beautiful, and I love you with all my heart."

"You don't have a heart," she said, and stormed toward Truscott.

"Here she comes," Truscott muttered. "Lord Jesus help me."

She pointed her finger at him. "You're supposed to be the ramrod, and I hired you to take my herd to Abilene, but that man was holding me against my will back there, and you didn't do anything about it! In fact, if my memory is correct—*you laughed!*"

"If you could see how funny you looked, you would've laughed too."

"I'm the boss around here, and you'd better get that through your thick skull! Next time I tell you to do something, by God, *you'd better do it!*"

"Damn women!" Truscott exploded. "Never leave a man alone! Nag nag nag—that's all they do, and there's no gittin' away from 'em! Wa'al I've had enough, you spoiled little bitch! You can go shit in yer hat and pull it down over yer ears! I quit!"

Truscott walked back to his horse, and she couldn't let him go. "Now just a moment . . ."

"I got nothin' to say to you! You ain't got a goddamn brain in yer head, and I'm tired of you naggin' at me!"

Truscott reached his horse and pulled down the stirrups. Cassandra caught up with him and grabbed the horse's bridle.

"I'll never get the herd up the trail without you. I'll be ruined if you leave."

He looked at her hand and muttered something, uncertain of what to do.

"Please," she said. "I don't mean to nag, but I'm not accustomed to seeing people kill each other."

"Git used to it," Truscott said. "It's all there is out here, and wait'll you see Abilene. You gotta promise you'll stay out'n my road."

"This is my herd, and you're my employee. You're supposed to do as I say."

"You hired me to ramrod this outfit, and that's what I'm doin'. Just 'cause you don't know nothin' 'bout nothin', that ain't my fault. I think all of us'd be a lot happier around here if you'd stop pokin' yer nose whar it don't belong. Are you gonna leave me alone, or am I ridin' out'n here, and don't think I won't do it!"

He was a tough old bird, and she saw indignation in his eyes. She'd wounded his ridiculous masculine pride again, but couldn't let him get away.

"I promise I won't put my nose where it doesn't belong anymore," she said. "If the men want to kill each other from now on, it's fine with me."

She heard hoofbeats, and saw squat Roberto riding toward her, bouncing up and down on his saddle, and hanging from his hand was his lasso covered with blood and gore. His gaze was on a distant mesa far beyond the herd, where he saw something receding forever.

"Party's over!" Truscott said. "Let's git to work!" He turned and walked toward Stone, thumbs in his belt. "Ready to ride?" he asked Stone.

"Ready as I'll likely be."

"Help 'im on his horse!"

Tomahawk watched as the cowboys carried John Stone toward him, and it was the first time he'd seen Stone close-up since the fight with the bear. Stone looked broken, with none of his usual spring and bounce, more dead than alive. Stone tried to raise his leg over the saddle, but it wouldn't go. Slipchuck lifted his ankle, and finally Stone slid into the saddle. Pain shot through him as he landed. He looked at his shirt, but no blood showed.

"You okay?" Slipchuck said.

"I smell that fucking bear."

"We got him on our boots." Slipchuck pointed to the soft greasy sheen on the tips of his tooled Mexican footwear.

Truscott sat on his chestnut stallion and pointed toward the northeast. "Colton's thataway! We'll meet by the Double Fork tonight! Try to keep yer no-good worthless asses out of trouble!"

Cassandra approached on her palomino mare.

"Don't take any chances," she said to them, "and for heaven's sake, don't get drunk."

Slipchuck raised his nose in the air. "Ma'am, whatever makes you think *we'd* do *that*."

"Because you're all drunkards, and everybody knows it, but you've got a job to do. Are we all clear on that?"

"Yes, ma'am," they replied sullenly.

She looked at Stone. "Do you think you'll be all right?"

He managed a wink. "They say whiskey has medicinal properties."

An expression of exasperation came over her face, and she

pushed the brim of her hat back. "Killing and drinking is all you know, but please stay sober until we get to Abilene, and then I promise I'll throw a party with all the whiskey you can drink, and you can kill each other with dynamite, for all I care."

Slipchuck leaned on his saddle horn. "You sure you can afford that much whiskey, ma'am?"

"You get my herd to Abilene, I'll afford it."

"You got yerself a deal."

Cassandra had misgivings as she watched them ride away, with Slipchuck in front, and Blakemore and Duvall flanking Stone. They weren't the most reliable bunch, but Slipchuck said he'd been in Colton before, and Truscott didn't dare send Mexicans, because they could be shot on sight in this part of Texas.

Cassandra watched John Stone slumped on his horse, and wondered if she'd made the right decision. The ride might open his wounds, but maybe a good doctor could save his life.

The cowboys had moved a substantial distance from her, and Indians could attack suddenly and carry her away. She touched her heel to the palomino's withers and trotted after the cowboys, her blond hair trailing in the wind.

She thought of four depraved degenerated cowboys lying on the floor of a saloon in Colton, when something caught the corner of her eye. Gouts of blood dotted the prairie like roses, and a lump that looked suspiciously like a man's nose adorned the spine of a prickly pear cactus.

Every motion of the horse caused misery, and when Stone's mind wandered, he lost his grip on the saddle. His legs lacked the strength to hold on, so he clutched the pommel with his hands.

"We can rest if you want," Blakemore said, extending an arm to steady him.

"Take your goddamn hand off me," Stone said weakly. "If a man can't stay on his horse, he deserves to die."

Blakemore removed his hand, and Stone felt himself sagging to the side. He reached for the pommel, but his reflexes were delayed, and he fell to the ground, where he landed head first and was knocked cold. The others stopped their horses and climbed down.

They rolled him onto his back, his chest rose and fell with his breathing, and he had a new three-inch gash on his head.

"This man won't make it to town," Blakemore said. "We'll have to go back."

"Can't go back," Duvall said. "Need supplies."

"A man's life is more important than supplies," grunted Blakemore. "We can brang Stone back to the chuck wagon, then head on into Colton."

Slipchuck looked at fresh blood oozing out of the new wound. "You're right—this man'll never make it to Colton."

John Stone opened his eyes like two gray curtains rising ever so slowly. "I'm not going to die," he said. "We're headed for Colton."

"Lord," Blakemore said sadly, "have mercy on this man."

"What're we waiting for!" John Stone gasped. "Tie me on my horse, and let's go to Colton!"

The speech weakened him, and he closed his eyes. They lifted him onto his saddle and tied his legs together with one length of rope, and his hands to the pommel with another length. Then they mounted up, and Blakemore and Duvall rode on either side of Stone, as Slipchuck led the way to Colton, somewhere out there on the endless prairie.

Stone bent and twisted with every step Tomahawk took. His wounds felt torn open, and dizziness assailed him. The sun rose in the sky and baked the four riders as they plodded across a sandy basin that went on for several miles. On the other side of the basin, they came to a water hole.

"We can break here," Slipchuck said, "but keep yer eyes open fer injuns."

They climbed down from their horses, then helped Stone to the ground. He staggered bowlegged to the water hole, dropped onto his stomach, and plunged his face into the cool, clear water. A little tadpole swam beneath a rock, and he wondered how it got here, across all those hills, through so many valleys. He gulped water, washed his face, and lay on his back, letting the sun warm his face.

"Water hole looks familiar," Slipchuck said. "Think I been here before." He looked around, sniffed the air, and said, "By the great pointy-toed Jesus!"

He jumped to his feet, ran from one side of the water hole to the other, then disappeared over a rise. A few moments later they heard his voice. "Look at this!"

Blakemore and Duvall drew their guns and ran after him, while Stone shuffled behind them, trying to pull his Colt out of its holster, but it was too heavy. He came to the top of the rise and saw Slipchuck standing with his hat off beside a pile of rocks.

"Boys," he intoned solemnly, "say hello to Guthrie. We was pards, but the injuns got him. I buried him here with me own hands, and it's good to see him again after all these years."

Slipchuck got down on his knees and clasped his hands together in prayer, while Blakemore and Duvall watched cautiously for signs of Indians. Slipchuck murmured a silent prayer, then crossed himself and rose to his feet. "So long, Guthrie ole feller. I'll stop by if I ever pass this way again." He pulled on his battered old hat and suppressed a sob that sounded like a goose choking to death. "The man whose grave you're lookin' at," he said to the others, "had a real talent that you don't see every day of the week. He knew how to find the cheapest whorehouse in every town from the Mississippi to the Rockies, he'd head straight fer it, and I never seed him go wrong. Miss 'im with all my heart, because you know, sometimes you come to a town and they moved the whorehouse, and you don't know whar the hell it is. Guthrie here could sniff 'em out like a coyote after a prairie hen. And I never saw a man who could cut a whore's price in half so easy. He had the gift, you might say. He'd say her tits was too small, or her ass was too big, or she didn't have enough teeth and she wasn't wuth the full price. Goddamn, when they made old Guthrie here, they throwed away the mold."

"How'd he die?"

"With the worse case of clap you ever seed, but that weren't what killed him. It was an injun arrow, dipped in skunk piss. We best fill the canteens and git a move on. Want to be back to camp by nightfall!"

They returned to the horses and tied Stone into his saddle. Then they rode northeast, heading toward Colton. Stone looked at Slipchuck, and realized Slipchuck had been everywhere, done everything, and was a walking breathing history of the frontier.

Blakemore rocked back and forth in his saddle as he said, "That grave back there reminded me of the *segundo*. You fellers ever think about what happened to him?"

Slipchuck looked Blakemore in the eye and replied, "Don't talk about it, don't think about it, and don't dream about it, becuzz it ain't fer us to know."

Slipchuck spurred his horse, and returned to his position as leader of the small band. They passed through a narrow defile with tall straight rock bluffs on both sides, an ideal spot for an ambush. No sunlight shone in the murky bottom, and they rode along with rifles in their hands.

At its end was a rolling plain with bald knobs and buttes, and they plodded across it, sweat dripping down their faces, but it was easier than working the herd. They didn't have to chase recalcitrant cows, and didn't eat the dust of the drag. At one in the afternoon they came to the crest of a hill and saw a cluster of buildings in the valley with a stream running through it.

"Colton," Slipchuck said. "Right on the nose. I said it once I said it a hundred times—if a man can see the sun, he can find anythin' he wants." He turned around in his saddle and looked at Stone. "How you doin', pard?"

Stone wanted to say he was all right, but was unable to get the sound out. He felt as if an elephant had danced on him, and his bones were crushed to jelly. He wanted to lie down and close his eyes.

They descended the incline, and Colton was four unpainted shacks, weathered and gray. Stone imagined a glass of whiskey sitting on a bar, and licked his lips mindlessly. Sometimes a glass of whiskey could do a man a world of good. There was no main street, and one of the buildings wore a sign that said:

PERSEVERANCE SALOON & GENERAL STORE
God Helps Them
That Helps Themselves

"Just remember, boys, we ain't here to git drunk," Slipchuck said.

"One little drink won't hurt nothin'," Blakemore replied.

"Mebbe one," Slipchuck told him, "but that's all. We gave our word to Mrs. Whiteside, and we can't let her down."

They stopped in front of the saloon, and Blakemore and

Duvall helped Stone off his horse. There was a hitching rail, but no sidewalk. Slipchuck opened the front door of the saloon.

A thin man with slicked-down black hair came from behind the bar and held out his hand. "Howdy, men—glad to see yez. Name's Handy—Milam Handy. Ain't seen a soul all day. What can I do fer yez?"

"Need supplies." Slipchuck said.

Stone limped to the bar and dropped heavily onto a stool. "Whiskey," he croaked.

Handy looked at him. "That man looks like he's 'bout ready to give it up."

"Fought a bear and the bear won," Slipchuck said. "Give us all a drink, and by the way, you got a sawbones 'round here?"

"Dr. Weatherford, but he rode out this mornin' fer the Bar Z, and ain't come back yet."

Stone watched the glass in front of him fill with whiskey. His tongue hanging out of his mouth, he reached for the glass, raised it with a trembling hand, and carried it to his lips. He sipped, and it tasted like turpentine. A wave of dizziness struck him, and he spotted a table against the wall. He staggered toward it and dropped onto a chair, not spilling one drop through the entire arduous journey.

Slipchuck handed the list of supplies to Handy. "How soon we git this stuff?"

"Take an hour or two to put it together."

"How far you say the Bar Z was?"

"Couple hours due north."

Slipchuck upended his glass, poured the contents down his throat, sighed, wiped his mouth with the back of his hand, and said, "We might as well try to find that sawbones, and leave Johnny here. You'll be all right, won't you, Johnny?"

Stone gazed at his glass. "Be just fine."

Slipchuck turned to Handy. "You'll look after him till we git back?"

"No trubble 'tall."

"If he wants another drink," Slipchuck said to Handy, "give it to 'im, but only one more, hear?"

"I'll take care of this man as though he were my own son," Handy replied stentoriously.

Slipchuck slapped Stone on the shoulder, and Stone thought

his shoulder would fall off. "Be back in a while, Johnny old boy. Don't fall in no shit."

"Won't be no trouble here," Handy said. "Hardly nobody ever stops."

Slipchuck, Blakemore, and Duvall walked out the door, leaving Stone alone with Handy. Stone stared at his three-quarters full glass of whiskey for a few seconds, thinking it was all his and no one could take it away. He raised it carefully to his lips and drank it down in three gulps. The whiskey hit him like a sledgehammer, and the room spun. His head fell forward to the table and he was out cold, making gurgling sounds in his throat.

Hardy went off duty an hour later, and such was his haste to get home to his dinner, he forgot to tell his replacement to look out for John Stone. The new bartender's name was Crenshaw, and when he saw Stone sprawled over the table, thought he was just another drunken cowboy, and Crenshaw had seen a million of them. Sitting behind the bar in a dirty white apron that covered his ample girth, he read a torn and wrinkled three-year-old newspaper, while Stone muttered and mumbled unintelligibly, his bearded cheek resting against old food stains and cigarette burns and the name of a woman, *Frisco Sal,* carved crudely into the surface.

Slipchuck, Blakemore, and Duvall came to the crest of a hill and saw a small black carriage shaped like a mollusk on the trail below. It was stopped, and the matching black horse grazed lazily on a clump of buffalo grass.

Slipchuck pulled his gun. "Looks like the sawbones had trubble."

He spurred his horse, and the others galloped behind him down the hill toward the carriage. As they drew closer, they saw a figure slumped in the front seat, still as death. They approached the carriage, and the horse raised his head to look at them. A chubby man with white chin whiskers was sprawled on the seat, wearing a derby, frock coat, and string tie. No arrows or bullet wounds showed on him, and a jug of whiskey rested on his lap, while a black leather bag sat near his feet on the floorboards. Slipchuck leaned closer to Dr. Weatherford, and smelled that special stench that only a severely drunken man exudes.

Slipchuck climbed down from his horse and stepped onto the running board of the carriage. "Doc?"

Dr. Weatherford, graduate of the Southwest Tennessee College of Medicinal Arts, last in his class, having delivered many into the world and assisted many more to their graves, didn't budge. Slipchuck took off his hat, touched his ear to the doctor's chest, and heard a steady beat. "He's just a little drunk," Slipchuck said. "You boys tie my horse to the back of this buggy, and I'll ride it into Colton. And while you're at it, keep yer hands off his goddamn jug!"

Stone opened his eyes and saw a different man behind the bar. He had no idea of the time, but an empty glass of whiskey sat in front of him. "Bartender," he groaned, "hit me again."

Crenshaw carried the bottle to the table and filled the glass. "Fifty cents," he said.

Stone stood unsteadily, reaching into his pocket, and it was empty. "My pards'll pay you when they git back."

Crenshaw removed the glass from the table. "I heerd that one before."

Stone watched with horror as the bottle moved away from him. "Wait a minute!"

"Whiskey costs money, mister."

"I'll trade you something."

"What you got to trade?"

Stone thought of his Colt, but didn't dare give it up. Then he remembered the genuine Indian hatchet stuck into his belt, for which he'd risked his life, for exactly this eventuality. He pulled it out and dropped it on the table. "Trade this for a bottle of whiskey . . . a fine specimen of Indian workmanship as you can see. Beadwork, feathers, inlaid precious stones. Folks back east would pay twenty dollars for it, but it's yours for only one bottle of whiskey, a bargain like this comes along once in a lifetime."

Crenshaw picked up the hatchet and looked at it skeptically. "Is that blood?"

"My blood."

"Who wants a hatchet with blood on it?" Crenshaw placed the hatchet on the bar. "Not interested."

"I'd settle for a half bottle."

"Don't want it."

"Tell you what. You pour me one good glass of whiskey, and this Comanche implement of war is yours."

Crenshaw thought for a few moments, shrugged, and poured the glass. Stone sipped some off the top, then carried the rest to the table, and pushed his old Confederate cavalry hat to the back of his head. He raised the glass to his mouth, drank some, and leaned back in the chair. This time he didn't want to be a pig and down every drop at once. This time he'd savor the rotgut, like a gentleman.

Whiskey killed the pain, and that's why he needed it. A pleasant warm glow radiated out of his abdomen, wreathed his heart, and calmed his mind. So what if a bear kicked the shit out of him? He'd survive.

He raised the glass again, and this time drained it dry. The glow burned brighter, and he leaned back in his chair. Crenshaw came out from behind the bar, carrying the bottle, and filled Stone's glass.

"Took a look at the hatchet, and it's worth more'n one glass of whiskey."

"You're an honest man," Stone whispered gratefully.

"You look like you been through a pile of shit."

"Tangled with a bear."

"I looked like you once,'bout five years ago down Mexico way."

"Bear?"

"Woman. Sixteen-year-old señorita to be exact, and I'll stack her against any two bears any day."

"I'll drink to that," Stone said.

Crenshaw poured. "It was back in Old Laredo, and she was the cantina owner's daughter. Now I might not look like much now, but in them days I was a desert rider with piss and vinegar in my veins. She was—I'll just come out and say it—the best fuck of my life."

"I'll drink to that," Stone said.

"So will I," replied Crenshaw, and he poured two more. "If I were smart, I would've stayed with her, and that cantina be mine now, but I was a crazy son of a bitch, and one night I had to screw her best friend in the kitchen. Everything was goin' just fine, but then Carmencita walked in, picked up a cast-iron frying pan, must've weighed ten pounds, and walloped me over the head with it, while I was a-tryin' to put me pants on. Look at this scar."

Crenshaw bent forward, parted his hair, and showed a wicked gash six inches long.

"I'll drink to that," Stone said, and Crenshaw poured again.

"And then," he said, pulling up his shirt, showing a shriveled patch of scar tissue on his belly, "she got her hands on a pot of hot oil. You might think I was unlucky, but she was a-aimin' fer me balls." Crenshaw looked out the window philosophically. "But I don't regret nothin', 'cause now when I'm alone at night, the fire in the stove's gone out, and it's a little cold 'neath my blankets, Carmencita's the one who keeps me warm."

"I'll drink to that," Stone said as his eyes glazed over and his head hit the table like a gong.

"Hey, Slipchuck, why don't you pass that jug up here?" asked Calvin Blakemore.

Slipchuck sat with the reins wrapped around his hands, and he glanced disapprovingly at Blakemore. "You don't steal a man's whiskey, you damned varmint. We got work to do."

"A little snort won't hurt, Slipchuck. If the sawbones drinks it, how bad can it be?"

"You can see what it's done for the sawbones. He ain't opened his eyes since we met him. I like my whiskey as much as the next man, but we got work to do."

"We'll do it better with a leetle whiskey."

Slipchuck heard something to his right, and swung in that direction in time to see Duvall's hand lift the jug out of the sleeping doctor's lap.

"Now just a minute!" Slipchuck roared. "I said no drinkin'!"

Blakemore and Duvall ignored him, dropping behind the carriage. Slipchuck craned his head around the black canvas roof and saw Duvall holding the jug to his mouth.

"Goddamn drunken no-good cowboys!" Slipchuck roared. "Wa'al, if you're gonna do it, I might as well join in! Pass that jug over here!"

Opening his eyes, Stone saw night had fallen; a coal-oil lamp burned atop the bar. He heard voices.

"I estimate three thousand head of mixed longhorns."

"How many cowboys?"

" 'Bout ten, but most of em's greasers. Looks like a real stove-up outfit. They even got a woman ridin' the drag."

"A woman ridin' the drag?" somebody asked incredulously. "What she look like?"

"Hard to see from a distance, but what could she be if she rides the drag?"

Stone turned his head to get a better look at them. They numbered nearly a dozen, and the lamp on their table illuminated their grizzled faces. They appeared to be men who lived in the open, and the one doing most of the talking wore a patch over one eye.

"Easy pickin's," he said. "We'll sneak up on 'em when they're sleepin', and . . ." One-eye dragged his forefinger across his throat. "They won't know what hit 'em. Then we'll shoot the night riders and take the herd. A piece o' cake."

"Nothin's ever a piece of cake."

"You're right on that," another voice said. "You remember the time we hit them pilgrims over in Rattlesnake Pass? You said them pilgrims'll never fire a shot in anger, but the damned Bible bashers blew so many holes in Buffalo Joe, why there weren't hardly nawthin' left of 'em. I'm still carrying lead in me left leg, and sometimes, after a long day in the saddle, I'm a-tellin' you, boys, it hurts."

Stone's face lay against Frisco Sal, the voices receded far away, and he drifted into the darkness.

"Their chuck wagon looks like a piece o' shit, but we should be able to git somethin' fer it. We can take turns with the wench, if'n she's not too ugly."

Stone straightened, burped, placed his fists on the table, pushed hard, and rose to his feet. Adjusting his hat low over his eyes, he stumbled toward the door, but his legs were shaking and black ink filled his eyeballs. The room tilted to the side, and next thing he knew he was on the floor. He tried to raise himself, but his elbows buckled and he collapsed unconscious onto the floorboards.

One-eye turned to him. "What the hell's that all about!"

Crenshaw the bartender held out his hands. "Can't hold his liquor, I guess."

"Who the hell is he?"

"Saddle tramp."

One of the rustlers said, "I'll see if he's got anythin' on him."

"You don't steal from a man wearin' a Confederate cavalry hat," Crenshaw replied.

"Probably ain't his."

"Leave 'im alone," said one-eye. "We got work to do."

The rustlers finished off their remaining whiskey, hitched up their gunbelts, and walked toward the door, stepping over John Stone's limp body.

It was dark when the black carriage rolled into Colton, and a lone light shone from the window of the Perseverance Saloon. Slipchuck brought the carriage to a stop in front of the hitching rail, turned to the doctor, and grabbed his lapels.

"Wake up, sawbones!"

Dr. Weatherford opened one eye, and his jowls were covered with a three-day growth of gray beard. "Who the hell're you?" he mumbled.

"Slipchuck's m'name, cows is m'game. We got a sick friend in that there saloon, and you got to help him."

"You got money?"

"Damn shore have."

"I can help him."

Dr. Weatherford lifted the medicinal jug out of his lap, took a few swallows, then adjusted his derby and climbed down from the carriage. Slipchuck, Blakemore, and Duvall followed him into the saloon. They pulled the door open, and saw John Stone passed out in the middle of the floor. Crenshaw sat behind the bar, reading his out-of-date paper.

"It says here we bought Alaska. Now what in the hell do we want Alaska for? Ain't nothin' there 'cept snow and ice, and the damn fool government spent seven million dollars for it! That's where yer tax money goes, boys!"

Blakemore and Duvall picked up Stone and laid him on one of the tables.

"You'll have to take off his clothes so's I can examine him," Dr. Weatherford said, lifting the jug to his lips.

Dr. Weatherford staggered from side to side, while Blakemore and Duvall struggled with Stone's clothes. Slipchuck lifted the jug from the doctor's hands and took another swig.

"Git headaches," Slipchuck said, "and sometimes see pink gophers."

"Know the feeling," Dr. Weatherford said with a burp. "Happens to me every day."

Finally Stone lay naked on the table, his body covered with gashes and bruises. Slipchuck, Blakemore, and Duvall stepped out of the way, and Dr. Weatherford cleared his throat, then removed his frock coat and rolled his soiled sleeves to his elbows. With an air of majesty, and still wearing his derby, the graduate of Southwestern Tennessee College of Medicinal Arts, last in his class, approached Stone and looked at him gravely.

"Looks like he fell off a cliff."

"Run into a bear."

Dr. Weatherford felt Stone's pulse and said, "Mmmm." Then he pressed his ear to Stone's chest. "Appears to be alive." Dr. Weatherford's filthy fingernails probed various portions of Stone's anatomy. He bent closer to take a better look. "Mmmm."

He turned to his black medical bag and removed a small black leather case about a foot long. He opened it, and inside was a saw.

"I'll have to amputate that leg, if you want to save this man's life."

Slipchuck, Blakemore, and Duvall looked at Stone's leg. "What's wrong with it?"

"Suppuration. You hold his left arm," he said to Duvall, "and you hold his right arm," to Blakemore. Dr. Weatherford blinked as he tried to focus on Slipchuck. "You sit on his leg."

"Now jest a minute," Slipchuck said. "You can't cut off a man's leg jest like that."

The doctor narrowed one eye and placed his hand on Slipchuck's shoulder. "My good man, I've been a doctor for thirty-seven years, and I've amputated more legs than you ever dreamed of. Now if you'll please get out of my way . . ."

Slipchuck looked at Blakemore, and Blakemore looked at Duvall.

"D'ruther be dead than have just one leg," said Duvall.

Dr. Weatherford turned to him. "It's easy for you to say, because you're not in danger of dying. But this man is. If that leg don't suppurate, I'll burn my medical diploma. This man won't live, less'n we act fast. Why, you can see he's out like a light.'

Dr. Weatherford walked toward Stone, holding the hacksaw by its leather grip, and at that moment Stone opened his eyes. The hacksaw gleamed in the light of the lamp, and Stone saw Dr. Weatherford, Slipchuck, Blakemore, and Duvall. "What's going on?" he asked weakly.

"It'll hurt for a while," Dr. Weatherford said, "so I'd advise you to bite down hard on this."

He rammed a piece of wood into Stone's mouth, and Stone spit it out. "What's going to hurt real bad?"

Dr. Weatherford looked down at him with his best bedside manner. "My boy, I'm sorry to tell you this, but your leg must be amputated without delay, otherwise you'll die of blood poisoning." He picked up the wood, wiped it on his greasy pant leg, and stuffed it into Stone's mouth again. "Hold 'im steady, boys! Once I amputated a leg in forty seconds!"

Stone reached for his gun, but was buck naked. He struggled to rise from the table, but the doctor pushed him down. "Be a man," he said. "I've had children gave me less sass than you. Now hold 'im steady, boys. I ain't got all day. The Travis woman is supposed to pop one tonight, and old Doc Weatherford has to be there to brang another young cub into the world."

Duvall scratched his stubbled cheek. "Don't believe much in doctors myself. D'ruther take my chances than have an old drunk saw my damn leg off."

"Now see here!" said Dr. Weatherford indignantly, raising himself to his full height. "I'll have you know there are more healthy one-legged men in this county than anywheres else in this great land of ours. Why, just the other day, old Clem Taylor says to me, 'Doc, I owe everythin' I got to you.'"

Stone rolled off the table and fell on the floor. As he struggled to stand, something nagged in the back of his mind. He wondered what it was, while reaching for his pants. "Nobody's cutting my damn leg off," he mumbled.

Dr. Weatherford's professional dignity was hurt, and he ceremoniously unrolled his sleeves. "That'll be five dollars!"

"You ain't done nothin'!" Slipchuck protested.

"My time is valuable, sir, and you brought me all the way

here for no good purpose. Why, there might be some other poor soul out there who needs his appendix pulled out, which I don't have to tell you is an extremely delicate medical procedure," he said, and took another swig.

Slipchuck paid him, and the doctor bit the coin to make sure it was genuine. Then he dropped it into his pocket and picked up his jug.

"A man's gotta rustle up a livin' anyways he can," the doctor said as he headed toward the door.

Stone's ears perked up. *Rustle.* He looked around the saloon, and his eyes fell on the round table in the corner. It all flooded back, and he staggered toward Slipchuck, who was examining the supplies they were supposed to bring to the camp.

"We've got to warn them!" Stone uttered.

Slipchuck picked up a bag of beans. "Have a seat, Johnny. We'll be a-leavin' in jest a few minutes."

Stone nearly fell on him as he grabbed his shoulders. "I was sitting over there, and I heard a gang of rustlers say they were leaving to steal our herd!"

Slipchuck pointed his finger at Stone's nose. "I've told you once, I told you a hundred times—you got to stop drinkin'. It's ruinin' yer mind, boy."

"I heard it, I tell you! The outlaw boss had a patch over his eye, and they were a hardcase bunch!" Stone turned toward Crenshaw the bartender. "Didn't you see a man with a patch over his eye, sitting over there with about ten others?"

"They was there all right."

Slipchuck looked at the bartender. "Did you hear 'em say somethin' 'bout cattle rustlin'?"

"Nope."

Slipchuck turned to Stone. "Like I said, Johnny. You got to leave the firewater alone."

Stone wavered and gripped the edge of the table. *I'm so goddamned drunk I can barely see. I've ruined my mind, and I'm imagining things.* A wave of despair and self-disgust ran through him. *I'm so drunk I nearly just got my leg sawed off.*

Slipchuck weighed a bag of coffee, to make sure the Triangle Spur hadn't been cheated. Crenshaw stepped out from behind the bar. "You ast me before if I heard them fellers talkin' 'bout rustlin', and in truth I din't, but that was one slimy crew of owlhoots, you ask me. I heard 'em arguin' about whether to rob yer friend here when he was passed out cold on the floor. Wouldn't be surprised if the one with the eye patch was Monty Kendrick hisself, and he's wanted for murder, robbery, rustlin', and every other damn thing you can think of."

There was silence for a few moments. "Looks like we got some hard ridin' to do," Slipchuck said. "Let's load them supplies and hit the goddamned trail."

6

THE FOUR RIDERS leaned into the wind that washed their faces and creased the brims of their hats. Slipchuck rode in front, and behind him was John Stone flanked by Calvin Blakemore and Luke Duvall. The horses' pounding hooves shattered the stillness of the night, and the riders were sheathed in moonlight, as furtive little prairie animals watched the eerie spectacle from behind bushes and trees.

The three-quarter moon shone overhead, and a few flimsy clouds floated across the starry heavens. In the distance, the outlines of a mountain range could barely be perceived. The rustlers had a two-hour lead.

Tied to his saddle, John Stone tried to hang on. Whiskey and wounds pushed him into semiconsciousness, and it was like a dream, or a nightmare. Every movement of his horse sent pain rocketing through his body, and hoofbeats tattooed his brain. His shirt was wet, and he looked at the widening stain—hard riding had opened his wounds. He thought about Cassandra, Truscott, and the others asleep around the campfire, and the rustlers sneaking up on them, to cut their throats. He clutched the pommel of his saddle as Tomahawk streaked over the grass, heading for the cow camp in the hills.

Cassandra opened her eyes; the *segundo* sat a few feet away, staring into the night. His head made slow, sweeping movements as he scanned the perimeter of the campsite.

Cassandra had seen the *segundo* on previous nights, guarding the campsite. He seemed to require no sleep, his skin was a peculiar shade of purple, and something terrible had happened to his mind.

He submissively followed any order that was given him, his will destroyed, a massive hulk with a big round head, sitting hatless on a rock, peering suspiciously into the darkness.

Five hundred yards away, the rustlers gathered around one-eyed Monty Kendrick as a night bird cried nearby.

Kendrick's face was shadowy in the darkness, and his black eye patch looked like a hole through his head. "You stay with the horses," he said to one of them. "The rest foller me, and we don't want no gunplay if we can help it. When I give the word, you know what to do."

Kendrick drew his knife, and the blade was eight inches long, flashing in the moonlight. He moved toward the campsite, and his men followed, to murder the sleeping cowboys where they lay.

Stone felt as though he was becoming unraveled. Black ink filled his eyes, his nervous system clicked off, and he sagged sideways in his saddle. Tomahawk felt the imbalance immediately, and slowed down as Calvin Blakemore reached out and caught Stone's shirt before Stone hit the ground.

The horses stopped in the shadow of a mountain, while rolling hills spread out before them in the dim moonlight. The cowboys climbed down from their saddles and untied Stone, then eased him toward the ground, where he lay unconscious.

"He's bleeding," Blakemore said to Slipchuck.

"Cain't leave him here," Slipchuck said. "'Coyotes'll git him fer sure. Tie him head down over his saddle."

He pulled the lariat down, while Blakemore and Duvall draped Stone over the worn leather. Slipchuck tied Stone's ankles and wrists together, then lashed his torso to the pommel.

"Won't be too comfortable," Slipchuck said, "but neither are coyotes. I figger the camp is only about a half hour away. Let's git movin', boys! There ain't much time!"

On a rock beside the charred remains of the campfire, the *segundo* sat still as a statue, staring blankly at the horizon, no expression on his filth-caked purple face. Everyone else was asleep, and the only sound was an occasional snore, murmur, or groan.

The *segundo* turned his head and made a deep, barely audible gurgle. He listened for a few moments, then stood and pulled out his gun. Crouching, peering ahead, he moved silently into the wilderness at the edge of the campsite.

Carrying their knives, the gang of rustlers moved across the prairie, their unshaven faces shadowy and sinister in the wan moonlight. They'd wait for Kendrick's signal when they reached the edge of the campsite, then move in for the kill. The main thing was cover your victim's nose and mouth, so no sound would escape as you ripped his throat from ear to ear.

Kendrick thought about the big payoff in a few weeks when they'd unload the herd. Every man would have a thousand dollars in his pocket, and they'd go to Mexico, live like kings until it was gone.

Kendrick had gathered them from the four corners of the frontier, men who found it easier to kill and steal than work and save. He thought of his favorite whorehouse in Mexico, with big feather beds and women wearing ball gowns with nothing underneath. He'd hire two of them and let them work him over, while he laid on his ass and smoked a cigar.

A shot rang out, and a bullet hole appeared suddenly in the middle of Kendrick's forehead. His one eye wide open and staring, he fell like a tree chopped down by a lumberjack. The last thing he saw was an image of himself in bed with two whores.

The *segundo* charged into the campsite, his gun still smoking. Cassandra and the cowboys were on their feet, guns in hand.

"Unnh!" said Braswell, pointing behind him. "Unnh."

"Somethin's out there," Truscott said. "Let's see what it is."

The *segundo* shook his head vigorously. "Unnh."

"Out of my way, you goddamned idiot."

Gun in hand, Truscott walked into the wilderness, followed by Cassandra and the cowboys. Ephraim jacked a round into his rifle as he brought up the rear. They advanced cautiously, and then Diego shouted, *"Aquí!"* He was on his hands and knees, holding Kendrick's head by his hair. "Anybody know the son om a beetch?"

"There's more prints over here!" said Ben Thorpe, the wrangler.

Truscott examined the ground. " 'Bout a dozen of 'em. They was headed for our campsite, and they was a-gonna massacre us."

A chill came over Cassandra. Diego was on his knees, studying the tracks. "That way!" he said, pointing into the darkness.

"Unless I miss my guess," Truscott said, "they're a-gonna try to stampede the herd! Git the horses!"

Slipchuck raised a hand, and the horses came to a stop in an arroyo bordered with cottonwood trees. He paused to listen, and shots could be heard in the distance.

"I think we'd better leave Johnny here," he said, "and one of you'll stay with him."

"Not leaving me anywhere," Stone whispered, bent double over his saddle. "Want to sit on my horse like a man."

Blakemore replied, "Last time you sat on yer horse, you damn near fell on yer head."

"Can do it," Stone wheezed.

"The more of us the better, I s'pose," Slipchuck said. "Untie him, boys!"

They removed the rope from Stone's hands and ankles, and Stone slid out of his saddle. "Where's my hat!"

Blakemore held it out and Stone placed it crookedly on his head.

"Sure you can ride, Johnny?" Slipchuck asked.

"Don't leave me behind, pard."

"Ain't never left a pard behind in me life." Slipchuck turned and listened to more gunshots in the distance. "Sounds like business is a-pickin' up, boys. We best git movin', or we'll miss the fun!"

The cowboys and vaqueros ran toward their horses as gunfire pealed across the prairie, the rustlers stampeding the herd. Cassandra placed her foot in a stirrup and elevated herself to the saddle of her palomino mare.

"Where the hell you goin'!" Truscott hollered, coming alongside her.

"With you!"

"We don't need no women in our goddamned road!"

"*You* get the hell out of *my* goddamned road, Truscott!"

She spurred her horse, and the animal sprang away from the speechless ramrod. *Son of a bitch,* thought Truscott. *Women're supposed to take cover when there's lead around, but this one's got gunpowder in her veins.* Truscott urged his chestnut stallion forward, while ahead of him in the night he saw Cassandra draw her gun. Her long blond hair trailed in the breeze as she raced across the prairie like an injun squaw looking for scalps.

The cattle were in full stampede, tongues hanging out and hooves hammering the ground. Behind them, rustlers whooped and fired their guns as they tried to keep them bunched and pointed toward their hideaway range. They'd stolen a herd, and now all they had to do was keep it.

The rustlers were a disciplined fighting unit, and most had been soldiers of one stripe or another during the war. Raggedy-ass cowboys wouldn't risk their lives for another man's cattle, and a hard charge was all it usually took to disperse them.

Four raggedy-ass cowboys on horseback suddenly appeared, guns in their hands. The rustlers aimed a barrage of lead at them, and the cowboys veered away, becoming indistinct in the dust and darkness. It appeared that one of the rustlers had scored a hit on a cowboy, and he was falling out of his saddle.

Stone was the cowboy, and he hadn't been hit, but he was barely conscious, his fingers limp as boiled macaroni. Tomahawk tried to stop, and Stone toppled to the ground, rolled over, and landed on his back, his shirt soaked with blood.

"I'm . . . alright," Stone muttered. "Help . . . me . . . git . . . on . . . my . . . horse."

"Man's dead," Slipchuck said, "but he won't lie down. Somebody'll have to stay with him."

Blakemore nodded as new gunfire broke out in the distance. "Sounds like Truscott and the others finally caught up with 'em."

Slipchuck and Duvall rode off on their horses, leaving Stone on the ground, with Blakemore kneeling beside him. Stone felt permanently fused to the earth, and he was sure he was going to die.

"Do you remember that Gypsy in San Antone?" he said in a whisper.

"Sure, but you ain't thinkin' . . ."

"She said I'd die young, and I can feel that bitch creepin' around here now."

"She told me I'd die young too, but I'm still here and the only thing creepin' around is rattlers."

"Dig me a deep grave, so the coyotes don't git me."

"No coyote would want you,'cause you'd stink too bad."

But on the rim of the next mesa the lobos already were gathering, and thought it smelled just fine. Whenever man's thunder sounded, they knew it meant a good meal. From all the surrounding territory they came, sniffing that peculiar essence of angry humans. Their long tongues licked over their teeth and snouts as they waited nervously in the moonlight.

The rustlers and cowboys galloped toward each other as the herd thundered off across the dirt and clumps of grass. The air filled with whistling bullets and shouts as men shot at each other in the light of the moon. The rustlers expected the cowboys to break and run before their firepower, but the cowboys and vaqueros kept coming, showing no sign of giving up the cattle without a fight.

Cassandra rode in the midst of her cowboys, gun in hand. She knew she might be killed, but there was no turning back now. The rustlers rode closer, aiming their guns while bouncing up and down on their saddles. Cassandra sighted down the barrel of her Colt at an unshaven rustler with a hatband made of wildcat teeth. She felt the shock wave of a bullet passing her cheek, and another bullet parted her hair. She fired a shot at the unshaven rustler, but he kept coming toward her, aiming his gun at her breast. She ducked, his gun fired, then a dark splotch appeared on his shirt and he fell backward over his horse's tail.

Cassandra looked beside her and saw Don Emilio Maldonado, a smoking gun in his hand. "When you shoot, señora, do not miss."

A rustler in a blue bandanna charged toward her, and she pulled her trigger when he was six feet away. His eyes rolled into his head, he sagged to the side and dropped out of his saddle. She turned to Don Emilio.

"Muy bueno, señora."

Cowboys and rustlers rode through each other's ranks, but it was hard to aim accurately amid the pitching and rolling of the horses. In seconds the surviving rustlers were behind the cowboys, while bodies lay on the ground, and wolves' eyes glittered in the darkness.

Teague counted empty horses. A hard fight loomed, and he wasn't ready to stop lead for a few longhorns. "Retreat!"

A rifle bullet sliced through his throat. He gurgled blood and fell off his horse . . . for a few longhorns. And the wolves saw that the pack would dine well tonight.

"Let's git out of here!" one of the rustlers shouted.

The rustlers were outgunned, and rode for their lives. Two shadowy figures appeared on a hill in the distance. One was short and spindly. Slipchuck. The other was broad across the chest. Duvall.

"No time to rest!" Truscott shouted.

He and his men rode off into the night, leaving bodies of dead rustlers bleeding onto the buffalo grass, because they'd taken on the wrong bunch of cowboys.

Blakemore placed a cigarette between Stone's flaccid lips, then lit a match. Stone inhaled feebly, and the moon spun around the sky.

"Never thought I'd die with a Yankee in attendance," he wheezed.

"You ain't dying. Only the good die young, and you ain't that good." Blakemore's brow creased, and he turned around. "Somebody's comin'!"

Blakemore raised his rifle and pushed back the brim of his Yankee forage cap. Stone blacked out, the cigarette dangling from the corner of his mouth.

Teague held up his hand, and the rustlers pulled their horses to a halt as a cloud of dust enveloped them. "I see horses," he said.

The rustlers followed Teague's finger and saw two outlined against the moonlit prairie.

"Let's git 'em," Teague said, digging his spurs into his horse's flanks. "At least the night won't be a whole loss."

A shot was fired, and Teague slumped in his saddle. A rustler named Burkley screamed, clutching his stomach. He was sixteen years old, and left his daddy's farm in Nebraska to make a fast buck on the trail, but now he'd feed a wolf family in Texas. The other rustlers were confused, then Harris took command. "There's only two horses!" he hollered, and he'd served as a sergeant in the 15th Virginia, carried a good-luck rabbit's foot in his pocket, and sincerely believed in it. "That means there's only two cowboys! Foller me!"

Harris charged the spot where the rifle had fired, and the rustlers followed, sending forth a hail of bullets that forced Blakemore to duck his head. All that separated him and Stone from the oncoming riders was a gentle rise of prairie, and the rustlers were coming fast.

Then Blakemore heard hoofbeats behind him. Ephraim rode into view, pulled a rifle from its scabbard, jumped to the ground, and dived behind the rise.

"Was lookin' for the others, and heard shots here," he explained.

Ephraim and Blakemore raised their heads, held their rifles steady, and opened fire at the riders bearing down on them. The air filled with hot lead, and two rustlers were shot out of their saddles, but the others continued their charge. Stone desperately tried to pull his gun out of its holster, but his hand weighed a million pounds. Horses jumped over the rise, and Sergeant Harris aimed his gun directly at Stone.

It only lasted a moment, but for Stone it was an hour of waiting for the bullet, when Ephraim shot his rifle from the hip, and Sergeant Harris, late of the 15th Virginia, went down, a good-luck rabbit's foot only carries a man so far. And it all began with a bright idea in the wrong saloon.

The prairie was strewn with bodies, and the lobos moved in. It was silent now, the cowboys had carried their dead away, leaving the rustlers. With quick snaps of their powerful jaws, they tore the clothes off the rulsters, and dug their teeth into warm steaming guts. Whining, snorting, howling ecstatically, they gulped the meat down. One clamped on something hard and tasteless, and spit out Sergeant Harris's good-luck rabbit charm.

The lobos feasted on human hopes and dreams, and the rustlers would never again leave a track that anyone would follow. Tomorrow morning ants would pick the bones, then shifting sands would polish them to a white gleaming shine, and finally the bones would become dust. The nearby mountain said: *One day I will not be here either.*

7

CASSANDRA SAT ON the ground near the chuck wagon, and Stone lay beside her, unconscious. On the other side of the campsite, cowboys dug a mass grave. The cost had been high. Calvin Blakemore was among the dead, a bullet lodged in his chest, his eyes closed and a grimace upon his frozen features.

Cassandra was bone-weary, hair unkempt, clothes filthy, and she couldn't stop thinking about the rustler she'd shot last night. He'd been close enough so she could see his face when the bullet struck, and his features had wrenched horribly. Whoever he was, he'd been some woman's son, and maybe another woman's brother. Perhaps a good woman had shared her bed with him, or maybe nobody ever loved him, and he'd been an orphan cruelly buffeted by the world.

Cassandra had always been taught that a human life was sacred, yet she'd taken a life, and for what? But she knew if she hadn't shot him, he would've shot her. It had been kill or be killed, and she'd done what she had to.

She heard footsteps, and looked at Truscott approaching. "Grave's ready," he said.

She arose and followed him to the hole, where the other cowboys and vaqueros were congregated, hats in their hands. Even the *segundo* was there, his hands hanging limply down his sides as he stared unswervingly into the murky grave.

It was one big ditch, because they didn't have time to dig four separate ones. Cassandra came to the edge of the grave and looked at the four dead men lying on the ground. She'd sat around the campfire with them only last night, and now they were gone. Their corpses lay before her, grotesquely contorted by violent death, and not one was thirty. They'd hardly seen anything of life, and all they'd known was cattle.

Truscott cleared his throat and shot Cassandra a sharp look. He was telling her to get on with it, because there was work to be done. She clasped her hands in front of her face and said, "Dear Lord, please accept these four men into Your loving care, and give them the peace of Your mercy. They were good men, and I don't understand why You had to take them, but we accept Your judgment, O Lord."

"Throw 'em in the ground!" said Truscott, and then turned to Cassandra. "Want to talk to you," he mumbled.

She gazed into his sunburnt features. He shuffled his feet, cleared his throat, looked her in the eye, and said, "You got more balls'n most men I ever met. You're okay in my book." He turned abruptly and walked away. "Let's git saddled up, boys! We got work to do!"

Cassandra felt dazed. Ephraim appeared behind the chuck wagon, and Cassandra walked toward him with a new swagger in her gait. "Ephraim, do you think you could put John Stone in the wagon, where he'll be out of the sun?"

"Sure thing, Mrs. Cassandra. I'll do it right now."

"Watch him carefully, and if he needs anythin', please get it for him?"

"Don't you worry none, ma'am. I'll take care of him as if he were my brother."

"I appreciate all you've done, Ephraim. If it weren't for you, he would've died long ago."

"Just doin' my job, ma'am."

Ephraim watched the sway of her hips as she walked away. He'd heard that Cassandra'd shot a rustler. There was more to her than they'd ever dreamed back at the Triangle Spur. He lifted Stone in his arms, carried him to the chuck wagon, and laid him inside next to newly purchased sacks of beans, flour, and coffee. Then Ephraim returned to the back of the chuck wagon, and filled a pot with water. He placed the pot over the fire, and looked at cowboys riding toward the herd.

When the cowboys were gone, he returned to the wagon and pulled out his beat-up old carpetbag. Opening it, he pulled out four small leather pouches and laid them on the table. He took a pinch of powder from each of the pouches and dropped them into a cup, then poured water in. The powders dissolved, becoming invisible. He carried the cup into the wagon and knelt beside John Stone.

"You white piece of shit," he said. "You're too dumb to die."

He touched the tip of the cup to Stone's lips, and tilted some of the liquid into Stone's mouth. Stone twitched, and a second later opened his eyes to half mast. Above him, he perceived Ephraim through layers of gauze.

"You . . ." Stone said in a voice barely above a whisper.

"Thass right, it's me, Massa John."

Stone remembered the gun battle. A rustler held him in his sights when Ephraim appeared.

"You saved my life," Stone murmured.

"Don't git no ideas 'bout that," Ephraim said quickly. "Ain't nobody gonna kill you, you sickly son of a bitch,'cept me."

He held the cup to Stone's mouth, and Stone swallowed it down. It tasted like ordinary water, and moistened his dry throat.

"You ain't gonna die," Ephraim replied, "because I ain't gonna let you. I has to save your ass, if'n I wants to kill your ass." He leaned over Stone and looked into his eyes. "I gots the power, Massa John."

The liquid dribbled over Stone's tongue. Every swallow was a battle through the lump of pain in his throat, but he got it down.

"You jest go to sleep, Massa John. And when you wakes up, we gonna have us some fun. I'm gwine give you your rotten life back, and then I'm gwine take it away again, just like that!"

Ephraim snapped his fingers, laughed, and crawled out of the chuck wagon, to get more powders from his medicine bag.

A small group of cattle grazed peacefully in the hot morning sunlight. Licking the salt off her lips, Cassandra counted twenty-seven. She rode forward to see if they carried the Triangle Spur brand.

Sweat plastered her shirt to her body, and she stank to high heaven. She approached the cattle, and they looked at her wearily. They carried the brand of the Triangle Spur on their left haunches, and were worth nearly six hundred dollars in Abilene. She heard hoofbeats behind her, and wheeled her horse. Don Emilio Maldonado rode down the incline, his big sombrero hanging on his back, his black hair glistening in the bright sun. Cassandra remembered his grip on her arms when the two vaqueros dueled with lariats, and now she was alone with him, but she was armed. She lowered her right hand toward her gun.

He laughed, his teeth showing white beneath his thick black mustache. "Are you planning to shoot me, Señora Whiteside?" he asked, mischief in his eyes.

"I will if I have to."

"I heard you came here alone, and *La Señora* should never go anywheres alone, because of the Indians."

"No Indian'll get me, because I've got a fast horse."

"Do not be so sure, *señora mio*. The Indians—they have fast horses too. First they will tear off your clothes, and every brave in the tribe will have you until they're too tired, and after that, if you are still alive, you will become a slave, and work day and night at filthy jobs for the rest of your life. Please do not let that happen, señora, because that would trouble me very mucho. Come, I will help you with these cattle."

Cassandra and Don Emilio got behind the longhorns and swung their lariats through the air. Don Emilio said something in Spanish, and the hot dusty cattle moved sullenly toward the main herd. She looked at Don Emilio, and he sat easily in his saddle, slamming his lariat on the haunch of a longhorn. When the cattle were moving along steadily, Don Emilio eased his horse toward Cassandra. They were alone on a vast plain, and the sun was directly overhead.

"Señora, may I have a word with you, please?"

She looked at him coldly, hoping that would make him keep his distance. "What's on your mind, Don Emilio?"

"I am not good with words, señora, because I am only a poor caballero. I apologize for the other day, when I held you tightly against me, but I could not help myself. I know I behaved badly, but I swear on my mother I will never do it again. I am telling you this because I want you to become my wife, señora. You may meet men richer than I, who have read more books, and maybe even a few who are more handsome than I, though I doubt it"—he laughed—"but you will never find one who will love you better than I. I will protect and cherish you with all my heart forever."

There was silence, and the breeze whistled through the sage. "That was a beautiful speech, Don Emilio," she replied. "How many girls have you said it to?"

"I offer you my heart, and that is how you answer. You are a coldhearted gringa, and sometimes I wonder why I love you so."

"How many?"

He shrugged. "A few."

"More than ten?"

"It is possible," he said curtly.

"I'm flattered by your offer," she said, "even though you've made it to numerous other women, but I can't think about men right now. If I don't get this herd to Abilene, I might as well be dead."

"I will get your herd to Abilene as long as there is breath in my body, señora. Then, will you consider my offer?"

Cassandra couldn't imagine marrying a Mexican vaquero who lived in the wild brush country, but she said, "When we reach Abilene, I'll give you my answer."

The fragrance of simmering beans wafted across the campsite, and Stone opened his eyes. He saw a dark figure in white robes above him, the angel of death beckoning.

A cold sweat broke out on his forehead, because what if all those stories were true? Hell might really be hell, and he'd roast on a spit in an oven till the end of time for his selfishness, lust, cruelty, and faithlessness. Something touched him, and he looked up at the angel of death towering above him. Dizziness filled his brain, and he thought his time had come. He closed his eyes and wheezed, as the black night swamped over him yet again.

Not far away, hidden by a clump of sagebrush, a lobo watched the strange spectacle. He'd been looking for scraps of food, and stumbled upon Ephraim and Stone. Ephraim, dressed in white robes, chanted and rocked from side to side as he poured powder on Stone's wounds. Picking up a bone and a gold chain, Ephraim sang a strange old African song.

The lobo shook his head in confusion. It sent a shiver up his spine and made his fur bristle. With a low growl of distaste, he crept away through the underbrush.

When Cassandra returned to the campsite that evening, the fragrance of Ephraim's stew came to her nostrils. The Negro cook sat by the fire, stirring his big cast-iron pot. Cassandra pulled the saddle off her horse and carried it near the campfire, dropping it on the spot she'd sleep that night. The aroma of the stew drew her to the fire. Her stomach was so empty she had cramps.

"When do we eat?" she asked.

"Jest a few minutes more, Mrs. Cassandra," Ephraim replied.

"How's John Stone?"

"Restin'."

Cassandra climbed inside the chuck wagon, and saw Stone lying on the floor, wrapped in swathes of tattered white cloth. Ephraim followed her in, and crouched beside her on the hard floorboards.

"I wouldn't touch him, if'n I was you," Ephraim said.

"What've you done?"

"He was shiverin', so I covered him up."

"Where'd the cloth come from."

"It's mine."

"I never saw it before. What do you use it for?"

Ephraim looked uncomfortable.

"I just asked you a question."

"My religion," he said reluctantly.

"What religion is that?"

"The religion of my people."

"Do you believe in Jesus Christ?"

"Yes, ma'am, I sho' do."

"Let's pray silently for a few moments, shall we?"

Ephraim bowed his head dutifully, and Cassandra clasped her hands together. She asked God to save Stone's life, then jumped down from the wagon and walked toward the fire, as Ephraim took one last look at Stone. "You're in God's hands, but you're in my hands too, you white son of a bitch."

The cowboys lined up with their tin plates, and let Cassandra go first. Ephraim filled her plate with stew, dropped two biscuits on top, and she sat next to her saddle, devouring the food hungrily, forgetting her New Orleans manners.

It was her first good meal since the last stampede, when all the food had been destroyed. Ephraim's stew was as good as anything she'd ever eaten in a New Orleans restaurant, the biscuits surpassed her mother's, and the coffee was thick and black, just the way she liked it. She scraped her plate clean, then returned to the pot and filled up again.

On the way back to her saddle, she noted a big black longhorn steer walking toward the campsite. He paused a few feet from the fire and mooed at Ephraim, who threw him a biscuit. The longhorn lowered his head and gobbled up the flaky sphere in seconds. His horns were unusual, one twisted forward and the other backward.

"Mr. Truscott," said Cassandra, "what's that steer doing here?"

"That's Old Ben," said Truscott, his mouth full of stew. "Ain't you met Old Ben yet?"

"What're you talking about?"

"You got nearly three thousand head of cattle," Truscott explained, "and every one of 'em is follerin' Old Ben here. Don't ask me how, but on every drive, there's one steer who's the leader, and Old Ben is it for this herd. Every morning we don't move until Old Ben here moves."

Truscott walked toward Old Ben, holding out his hand in friendship. Old Ben looked with big round bloodshot eyes at the lanky foreman as Truscott patted his head.

"It always pays to be pals with Old Ben," Truscott said. "Throw me one of them biscuits, willya, cookie?"

Ephraim tossed a biscuit to Truscott, who held it in his stiffened hand. Old Ben lowered his head and extended his lips gingerly around the biscuit, plucking it away. Truscott stroked Old Ben's ear and grinned. "Me and Old Ben, we're pards, ain't we, Old Ben?"

"What about when we get to Abilene?" Cassandra asked.

"Old Ben'll be first in the railroad car, and when he gets to St. Louis, first in the slaughterhouse, and they'll all foller him."

Old Ben nudged Truscott's leggins with his big black nose.

"No more for you," Truscott said. "You're supposed to eat grass. The biscuits is for us."

Truscott returned to his plate and resumed his meal, and Old Ben watched from afar for several minutes, then turned and rumbled back toward the herd.

"When I was a kid, on my first drive," Truscott said, "I actually saw the leader try to git into bed with the ramrod, busted half his ribs. You cain't git too friendly with 'em, boys. Got to show 'em who's boss."

Cassandra finished the meal and drained her cup of thick black coffee. Now all she wanted was bed. She washed her plate and cup in the bucket of water, then stopped by the basin and splashed water on her face and hands.

She walked back to the campfire, and in the distance a coyote howled, his stomach full of dead rustlers. The men sat around the flames, smoking cigarettes and drinking coffee, and she couldn't go to bed as long as they were awake. She was determined to show them she could do anything they did.

She sat by the fire and looked at the dancing flames. Beside her, Truscott pulled a plug of tobacco out of his shirt pocket and bit off a piece, then held out the plug to her. "Want some?"

Most cowboys chewed constantly, spitting everywhere, their mouths ringed with brown tobacco juice. "Don't mind if I do," she said.

She took the plug from Truscott's hand and dug her white teeth into it, but it was like tree bark. She growled and worked her jaws, and finally a piece fell off into her mouth.

She passed the plug back to Truscott, and it tasted sweet. Now she could understand why they liked it. It reminded her of an apple, but then suddenly something harsh and terrible slid down her throat, and she thought she was choking to death. Her eyes bugged out of her head and she coughed violently. Truscott leaned toward her and slapped her back.

The tobacco shot out of her mouth and landed in the fire, where it sizzled treacherously. Cassandra got to her feet and clasped her hands around her throat, staggering from side to side as she gagged and hacked. Somebody threw her a canteen, and the cowboys laughed as she gulped the water down. She stopped coughing, and wiped her mouth with her sleeve. Then she threw the canteen back.

Truscott winked. "Don't never put nothin' in yer mouth if'n you don't know what it is."

"Disgusting," Cassandra said. "Don't know how a person can chew it."

"Look how purty it makes yer teeth," he said. He drew back his gums, and in the light of the fire, his teeth were brownish yellow.

Cassandra felt herself being shaken. She opened her eyes and saw Diego above her, his hand on her shoulder.

"Night duty, señora."

Cassandra drew herself to a sitting position, and her mind was heavy with exhaustion. She couldn't see how she'd ever make it to Abilene on a schedule that permitted so little sleep. Longingly she remembered her big feather bed back at the Triangle Spur, where she'd slept peacefully through every night.

She rolled her blankets and carried them to the chuck wagon, placing them beside John Stone, who lay in his white cocoon, his features shadowy in the dimness. The big coffeepot sat on the blackened embers of the fire, and she poured herself a cup of the thick tepid liquid. Sipping, she looked at her cowboys sleeping in their blankets. A single spire sat on the distant horizon, illuminated faintly by the moon. *It's beautiful,* she thought. *I love this land.*

One cowboy wasn't asleep, and he was the *segundo*, sitting on a rock, a rifle in his lap. Cassandra finished her coffee, washed the cup in the basin, and headed for the remuda. Her night horse was her favorite palomino mare, Petunia. Raising herself into the saddle, she pulled Petunia's head gently toward the herd, and together they began their journey to the plain where the longhorns were sequestered for the night.

In the distance she saw the herd gleaming in the moonlight. She thought of Old Ben, who'd lead them into the slaughterhouse, and they'd most likely wind up on the plates of New Yorkers and Bostonians, or other people who lived in the East. At one time she'd envied those fancy people, with their opera houses, symphony orchestras, and exquisite restaurants, but not anymore. They lived opulent, but cramped lives, whereas she possessed the grandeur of a great land, with mountains that made the greatest cities look like petty squalid piles of trash.

She came to the edge of the herd, and the longhorns watched her warily. They still were jumpy from the many frightening experiences they'd endured since leaving the peaceful range near San Antone, so she sang them a plaintive lullaby that her mother taught her when she'd been a child. Her light soprano voice floated over the cattle and reverberated off the mountains, as the cattle lowed in the distance, and stars sparkled in the sky.

A figure rode slowly toward her out of the night, and her voice caught in her throat. Embarrassed, she sat straighter in her saddle as Slipchuck approached, for he was on night duty too, riding around the herd in the opposite direction.

He touched a long bony finger to the brim of his ruined cowboy hat. "Evenin', ma'am. Could I have a word with you?"

She pulled back the reins of her horse. "What's on your mind, Slipchuck."

He sniffed, spit a wad of tobacco juice, and appeared nervous. "I don't know how to say this, Mrs. Whiteside, but my 'sperience has taught me it's a strange world, and you never know what might happen. I been havin' me some thoughts about you, and thought I'd bring 'em out into the open and air 'em out, if you know what I mean. Now, I've seen it happen that there's some young women, such as yerself, who sometimes like the older man. Now I ain't sayin' you're feelin' that way about me, but if you are, I'd be right proud to accommodate you. I know I'm old enough to be yer caddy, but when my daddy got married, he was nearly my age, and my momma was thirteen. I'm still strong, I can shoot the eye out of a gnat at fifty paces, and I'm still good at other things too, if you git my drift. So if you're havin' any thoughts like what I'm talkin', we can git married in the next town, and the ramrod can be the best man."

Slipchuck looked at her hopefully, and she felt as if she'd been hit over the head with a broom. "I appreciate your offer," she said, "and I'm very flattered that you'd want to marry me, but I only just lost my husband, and I'm not ready to get married again. I hope you understand."

Slipchuck held up the palm of his hand. "You don't have to say no more. But you change yer mind, just gimme a holler."

Slipchuck winked, spat another gob of tobacco juice at the grass, and rode off, yodeling to the longhorns.

8

JOHN STONE OPENED his eyes, and the roof of the chuck wagon came into sharp focus. He was wrapped in white cloth, the pain was greatly diminished, and his strength had returned. Somehow, miraculously, he was himself again, and he knew who was responsible, and why. He crawled to the front of the chuck wagon and looked outside.

Ephraim was nearby, lighting the morning fire, a sardonic smile on his face. "How we feelin' today, Massa John?"

The cowboys and vaqueros spun around and stared at Stone with astonishment. There was silence as Stone jumped down from the chuck wagon and stood erectly, except for a few creaks in his bones, due to the long period of inactivity. Truscott took off his hat and scratched his head. The *segundo* bent forward and focused his unblinking eyes on Stone, and Stone knew they were brothers under the skin.

"I said it once, I said it a hundred times," Slipchuck declared. "God protects an honest cowboy."

Slipchuck placed his arm around Stone's shoulders, and together they walked toward the campfire, where Ephraim fried their breakfast steaks, the aroma of charred meat curling past their nostrils. Stone felt starved, a massive hollow in his stomach, and took his place in line.

The cowboys and vaqueros continued to stare at him, and he was ill at ease. Everyone knew Ephraim somehow had cured him, but nobody wanted to comment. Truscott cleared his throat and hitched his thumbs in his belt as he walked toward Stone.

"Glad to see you're feelin' better, Johnny. If'n you can ride today, we sure can use yer he'p."

Ephraim said, "Better let him rest up a couple more days."

Truscott wasn't about to argue with Ephraim, not about a goddamn thing. "Whenever you're feelin' up to it, Johnny, it's okay with me."

Meanwhile, Cassandra was returning from the latrine, wondering if there was some way she could cut her hair, because it was becoming the murky nest for a variety of insects, and carried all manner of filth within its golden strands. Maybe, if she lay her head on a log, one of the cowboys could saw her hair off with his knife.

She came to the clearing and headed for the chuck line, when her eyes widened at the sight of John Stone. He stood with the cowboys, and they all carried tin plates in their hands. At first she thought she was hallucinating, then moved toward him, her eyes narrowed in mystification. "Are you all right, Johnny?"

"Much better, Mrs. Whiteside."

Cassandra stared at him as though he were a ghost. The four-inch scar on his head was covered with a black scab, whereas it had been open and bloody last time she saw it.

"Brea'fass is ready!" Ephraim said.

Cassandra made her way to the front of the line, and wondered if she were dreaming. How could a man recover so quickly from such wounds? She held out her plate, and Ephraim dropped a cut of tenderloin atop it, with several biscuits. She filled her cup with coffee and carried everything to her saddle, where she sat down. The line advanced, and finally it was Stone's turn. Ephraim carefully placed an enormous steak upon it, and lay the biscuits to the side. "I made some special tea might he'p you, Massa John," he said.

Stone picked up the cup, and it was filled with medium brown liquid dotted with tiny black particles. It looked revolting, but he'd drink every disgusting drop. He made his way to a spot near Cassandra, cut off a gob of steak, and put it into his mouth. It was his first food in days, and he felt the taste explode throughout his body. Ephraim was taking good care of him so he could kill him, but he was in for a surprise. Stone knew Ephraim would be the one to die.

Stone looked at the other cowboys. "Where's Blakemore?"

There was silence for a few moments, then Truscott said, "Dead."

Stone's fork froze in midair. "How'd it happen?"

"Rustlers got him, and damn near got you too. We buried him yesterday."

The food went tasteless in Stone's mouth. The Gypsy hag in San Antone had told Blakemore he'd die young, and now he had. She'd said the same thing to Stone, and if she were right once, would she be right again? Stone looked at Ephraim, who smiled over the shimmering flames of the campfire. Stone's hand trembled for a moment, then he pulled himself together. "How'd he die?"

"With his boots on and a gun in his hand," Truscott said. "Hope I go the same way."

The cowboys finished breakfast, climbed onto their horses, and drifted toward the herd. Stone remained near the campfire, munching his second helping of steak. Cassandra was last to leave. "Ephraim," she said, "may I speak with you alone a moment?"

"Yes, ma'am," replied Ephraim, washing the plate that had held the biscuits. He wiped his hands on his apron and followed Cassandra to the far side of the chuck wagon, where no one could hear them.

Cassandra narrowed her eyes suspiciously as she looked up at Ephraim. "How'd you do it?"

"Do what, Mrs. Cassandra?"

"Somehow you cured John Stone, and you also did something to the *segundo*. How can you do these things?"

Something in his eyes frightened her, and she took a step back.

"Don't be afraid of me, Mrs. Cassandra," he said. "I'd never do nothin' to you. Old Ephraim's on your side."

She wasn't reassured. Something about him terrified her. "Bring up the chuck wagon soon as you can."

She walked toward her horse, and glanced at John Stone. He appeared almost as good as new, but yesterday had been at death's door. And the *segundo* was a walking corpse. She'd expected Indians and rustlers on the drive, but not this.

She climbed onto her horse and rode off with the cowboys. Stone finished the tea and returned the cup to the chuck wagon, where Ephraim was washing his big butcher knife. "Jest one more day, Massa John," he said, holding up the butcher knife, and a sunbeam kissed the sharpened point. "Know what I mean?"

Cassandra rode the drag, enveloped in dust and the stink of cattle. Ahead of her, the *segundo* chased an old cow back to the herd. Cassandra's back was sore, and the effects of inadequate sleep took their toll. She'd never worked so hard in her life, and had too much to worry about.

A figure rode toward her out of the swirling dust, and it was Don Emilio Maldonado, wearing his wide-brimmed sombrero. He was accompanied by Roberto, the vaquero who'd dragged Manuelo to death with his lariat.

"I have good news!" Don Emilio said, removing his sombrero and bowing from the waist. "You have been promoted to flank rider! Roberto here will take your place on the drag!"

"I thought," Cassandra said, "that the newest hand rode the drag."

"That is true, señora, but we are trying something different here. Please do as I say."

"I don't want to be treated any differently from anybody else," she told him evenly. "If we hire a new man, he'll ride the drag and I'll take the flank position."

Don Emilio became exasperated. "If you want to keep the men happy, señora, you will not ride the drag anymore. They do not want you here, and if you stay, they will become a pack of devils that no one can control. So please be a flank rider, I beg you. Report to Duvall, and he will tell you what to do."

Cassandra didn't want to upset the men, because everything was difficult enough as it was. "All right," she said, "but I don't like it."

His eyes sparkled. "If only you would let me kiss your foot, I would be happy for the rest of my life."

"I haven't washed my feet in three days, and we'd better find water tonight, because I need a bath."

"If I could bathe you with my own two hands, you would be cleaner than ever in your life."

She prodded her horse, and the animal moved away from Don Emilio and Roberto, who watched her recede into the dust kicked up by the sick and lame longhorns in the drag. Moving from dust to fresh clear air, she pulled down her bandanna so she could suck it into her lungs. She rode forward leisurely for several hundred yards, exulting in her newfound freedom, and then spotted Duvall.

"I'm the new flank rider," she said, "and Don Emilio said you'd tell me what to do."

Duvall pointed to the herd ten yards to his right. "Ain't much work at the moment. Herd's settled pretty good—guess they're finally gittin' used to the drive."

She couldn't help noticing, through his open shirt, the scar on his neck. She'd always wondered where he got it, but thought she'd be better off without the information.

"You know," Duvall said, "I been thinkin' 'bout you, all alone in the world like an orphan. A woman needs a man to look out for her, do the tough jobs that come up, know what I mean?"

"I had a man, and he was no damn good," she replied, and spat at the dirt.

"There's all kinds of men, Mrs. Whiteside. Some're varmints, and some're decent. Now you take John Stone, fer instance. You couldn't ask for a finer man. You and him'd make a good couple, you ask me. 'Course, he drinks too much, but a good woman's all he needs."

"He's in love with the woman in that picture he carries around."

"He'll git over her, 'specially if he had somebody else to keep him warm at night." Duvall winked. "I'd ask fer yer hand myself, but I'm already spoken fer. I'm a-gittin' married after this drive is over, to Miss Eulalie Parker of San Antone."

"Congratulations," she said. "Glad to hear it."

"You should be gittin' married too, because it ain't good fer a woman to be alone. Onc't you git that itch, you got to scratch it, and that's when a woman can git into trouble. John Stone is the kind of man you can rely on. If he says he's gonna do somethin', you can build a house on it."

The chuck wagon rolled over the plains, tipping from side to side, its frame trembling, and Stone rode twenty yards to its left, atop Tomahawk. The pain was nearly gone from Stone's body, and he was covered with healed scars. The bones in his chest that'd felt broken now were solid.

Stone saw Ephraim sitting on the box seat of the chuck wagon, reins wrapped around his big hands. Tomorrow morning they'd fight it out, and when it was over, one man would be standing and the other dead. Stone expected to be the man standing, with a bloody knife in his hand, or a Gypsy's curse on his gravestone.

Stone'd rather fall into a well, or get trampled by longhorns, than let the ex-slave kill him. *I didn't come through five years of war to let a nigra piss on my grave.*

It was evening at the campsite, and Cassandra had just finished dinner. It was time to go to bed, but first she wanted to cut her filthy tangled hair, and she'd even found a grasshopper in it that afternoon. God only knew how many days it'd been there.

On top of that, they hadn't found a water hole, and she didn't want to use precious drinking water for a bath. She stank the way her cowboys stank, sweat and horseshit, instead of the fine perfumes she'd worn in New Orleans, and had dirt in her ears and between her toes, unthinkable in the old days.

But the big problem was her hair. She was afraid to look in the mirror, for fear of what she'd see. Better get rid of it. She leaned toward Slipchuck and said, "Is your knife sharp?"

Slipchuck spat a gob of tobacco juice into the fire, where it sizzled and exuded a black puff of smoke. "Could split a skeeter's peter."

"Do you think you could cut off my hair with it?"

Slipchuck scowled. "Couldn't do that, ma'am. Hand's liable to slip, cut yer head off."

"Your hand's steady as a rock, Slipchuck. Do me the favor, will you?"

He shook his head and got to his feet. "Not me."

She turned to Truscott.

"I ain't no barber," he told her.

"It'll just take a minute, and you don't have to do a neat job."

"Nope."

She looked at Diego, the vaquero. "Will you help me, *amigo*?"

"You hair is beautiful the way it ees, señora. Why you want to fock it up?"

"It's dirty—can't you see?"

"When you ride in the sun, I see what Coronado dreamed when he looked for El Dorado."

Cassandra turned to Duvall washing his tin plate. "Care to help me out?"

"I like yer hair the way it is, Mrs. Whiteside. Sorry."

She looked at Ephraim, who stood near the fire, stirring tomorrow's stewed beans. "Ephraim, would you cut off my hair, please?"

Ephraim shuffled his feet. "If'n I cut off your hair, Mrs. Whiteside, your cowboys're liable to cut somethin' off'n me."

The cowboys chortled, and her eyes fell on Don Emilio Maldonado, leaning against his saddle, smoking a cigarette.

"How about you?" she said.

"I am very sorry, señora," he replied, "but I cannot do it. It would be a crime against God to cut such beautiful hair."

"You told me once you and your men would do anything I wanted, and you'd be my *slave*, is that correct?"

"Si, señora."

"You swore on your mother, I believe, is that not so?"

"Si, that is so."

"Then cut off my hair!"

"If I cut off your hair, señora, my vaqueros will kill me. They all love your hair, and so do I. You heard what Diego said—it reminds them of El Dorado. You are the queen of their hearts. How can you do such a crazy thing?"

"May I borrow your knife, please?"

He hesitated, but she darted forward quick as a minx and pulled his knife out of its scabbard before he knew what happened.

"Now, señora," he said, raising his hand in alarm.

"Stay where you are, Maldonado. Don't get in my road."

She threw her hat to the ground, raised her golden tresses in her left hand, and tried to cut through them with the knife in her right, but the knife wouldn't go through. She grit her teeth and pushed the knife harder, but all it did was pull at her roots and hurt.

She realized she couldn't do it, and was so mad she could spit. "You sons of bitches!" she screamed, hurling the knife at the ground with such force that it went in four inches.

The men burst into laughter. Cassandra placed both her

hands on her hips and stared at them. *If I were a man, I'd beat the shit out of them.* And the worst part was they wouldn't stop laughing. Several were actually rolling around on the ground. Don Emilio's face was red, and he appeared to be having convulsions. Slipchuck looked as though he'd have a heart attack. There they were, in the middle of nowhere, having a great time! They could fight, kill, and laugh too! They really liked her, they'd paid her a beautiful compliment, and she hadn't the grace to accept it.

She felt like thanking them, but they wouldn't play it that way, and neither could she. She put on her hat, tipped it to a rakish angle, and performed a direct Truscott imitation as she strolled away, thumbs in her gunbelt. "Wa'al, guess the old mop's stayin' on!"

She walked into the darkness at the edge of the campsite. Before her the Milky Way cut a diagonal swathe toward the three-quarter moon. Four buttes stood like sentinels in the distance, and she thought this moment was worth all the cattle in the world. No matter where she went, no matter what happened to her, no one would ever be able to take away this glorious night.

A figure loomed before her, and she went for her gun.

"It's me," said Stone.

"Thought you were an injun," she replied. "What're you doing here?"

"Look." He pointed at Old Ben lying a few feet away, chewing his cud.

She bent over and patted the bristly hair between the animal's weirdly twisted horns. "It's strange," she said, "that he'd rather be here with us than back at the herd with his own kind."

"He likes us," Stone replied.

She dropped to the ground, and Stone sat beside her. Old Ben looked at them peacefully with huge glowing eyes as drool dripped from his lips.

"I wonder what he has," Cassandra said, "that makes him the leader."

"They're afraid of him."

"Doesn't look scary to me. I'd say he's more of an eater and sleeper."

"Cowboys told me the bulls rip each other wide open with

their horns during mating season. I don't think they'd follow him if he wasn't a good fighter."

"Truscott told me he'll lead them right into the slaughterhouse. I wonder what he'll think when they kill him. Do you imagine he'll feel betrayed?"

"Heard a story once about a steer like Old Ben, and when they got to the railhead, the boss decided to save him from the slaughterhouse, because he'd done such a good job. The boss hired cowboys to drive the steer all the way back to Texas, and that steer'll probably live longer than you or me."

Cassandra brightened. "Maybe that's what I should do for Old Ben, if we get through to Abilene."

"We'll get through. There's nothing that could stop this outfit now."

Her face floated before him in the light of the moon, and her breasts strained against her dirty shirt. Her first two buttons were undone, and he could see the cleavage.

Her voice hit an odd note. "Think I'd better turn in. S'cuse me."

Stone looked up, and she was gone. He waited a few minutes, then rose and walked back to the campsite, leaving Old Ben lying on the grass, chewing contentedly, as dying wisps of smoke from the campfire floated through the air like incense. Stone washed his hands and face in the basin beside the chuck wagon, and heard a footfall behind him.

"Tomorrow mornin', Massa John," Ephraim whispered.

Stone turned and looked at the ex-slave. "I wouldn't miss it for all the gold in California."

"You'd better sharpen your knife fo' you go to bed, 'cause I already sharpened mine."

Ephraim stepped away, and Stone wiped his face with the community towel, which was gray with filth. He walked to his saddle, hung his hat on the pommel, sat, and pulled the Apache knife out of his boot. He ran his finger along the blade, and it was sharp as a razor.

He sheathed the blade and stretched out on the ground, pulling the blanket over him. Tomorrow, at this time, the sun would set on a fresh grave, and he hoped it wouldn't be his.

9

IT WAS DAWN, and the cowboys rolled out of their blankets as Ephraim led a steer into the encampment.

"Needs fresh meat this mornin'," he said.

The cowboys looked at him curiously. Usually Ephraim butchered cattle on the far side of the chuck wagon, but evidently this morning he was going to do it in front of them.

Ephraim turned the steer loose, and the animal looked around fearfully as Ephraim pulled his big butcher knife from the sheath on his belt. He cast a meaningful look at Stone, then came up behind the steer, wrapped his arm around the steer's neck, pulled back the steer's head, and slit his throat.

Blood geysered into the air, and the steer's legs buckled. The immense creature collapsed onto the ground, and Ephraim's knife sliced the hide easily, leaving long trickling red lines. He butchered the steer with smooth clean strokes, pulled out the warm guts, and then carefully, almost surgically, removed the loin.

He cut chunks of fat and threw them in the skillet, where they hissed and crackled over the flames. Then he lay the loin on his chopping board and cut several thick steaks as the fragrance of the beef fat permeated the campsite.

Stone knew Ephraim was sending him a message, but he was sure he could put Ephraim away. Well, he was almost sure. He cursed the night he'd visited the Gypsy hag in San Antone, because her curse lurked like an assassin in his mind.

"Come and git it!" Ephraim shouted, shaking his big black skillet full of steaks.

The cowboys lined up, and Cassandra took her place at the front. She'd lost her appetite, watching Ephraim butcher the steer, but the aroma of the cooking meat brought it back, and Ephraim dropped a thick juicy steak on her plate. She lifted a few hot biscuits from the dutch oven and sat on the ground near her saddle.

Stone stood behind Truscott in the line, and Truscott appraised him through slitted eyes. "You look like you can ride today, Johnny."

Ephraim's voice came to them from the fire. "Needs another day to rest up."

"Seems fine to me," Truscott said, appraising Stone's broad shoulders.

"Tomorrow," Ephraim said.

Truscott offered no argument. One more day wouldn't make that much difference.

The men ate quickly, washed their tin plates in the bucket, stacked them on the table, and walked toward the remuda. Stone reached into his saddlebags, pulled out his sharpening stone, and ran it over the blade of his Apache knife. He looked up at Ephraim, who washed the skillet.

"After I kill you," Ephraim said in a low voice, "I'll bury you in the ground, but not too deep, because I want the bugs and coyotes to get some of you. I'll tell the others you went off for a ride and never came back, and they'll figger the injuns jumped you."

Stone didn't say anything, because he intended to speak later with his knife. He sharpened the blade, and the scraping sound mingled with hoofbeats of horses as the cowboys and Cassandra rode toward the herd.

Ephraim loaded his gear into the chuck wagon, and closed the back. Then he sauntered toward Stone and sat a few feet away.

"You lookin' a little nervous, Massa John."

Stone continued sharpening his blade. The cowboys receded into the distance, and in another ten minutes would be out of sight. Then the fight could begin.

"Want to tell you somethin'," Ephraim said. "Back in Beulah Land, your l'il Marie girl loved my black ass—you know that?

She come to me in the fields at night, when dumb you was asleep in your bed, and we done all kinds of strange thangs, and let me tell you, she said to me onc't she'd never been loved by a white boy the way she was loved by me."

Stone forced a laugh, but it came out strangled. "You want to rattle me, but I don't rattle. I'll cut your throat the way you cut that steer this morning."

"If you not rattled, Massa John, how come you talkin' so funny?" Ephraim looked in the direction the cowboys had gone. "We best wait a few more minutes, to make sure none of 'em comes back. We don't want to be interrupted, do we, Massa John?"

"Take your last look at the world, because you're a dead man."

"I should thank God,'cause He's given me you to kill." Ephraim got on his knees, clasped his hands together, and prayed. A flock of singing birds flew overhead, and a wild dog barked in the distance. Ephraim rose to his feet and pulled his butcher knife out of its sheath. "I think we can git started now, Massa John."

Stone reached to his boot and pulled out his Apache knife, his old Confederate cavalry hat slanted over his eyes, while Ephraim was bareheaded, tiny beads of sweat glistening on his forehead. The sun rose in the sky behind them, and the cowboys were gone.

Stone and Ephraim looked at each other, blades shining. Ephraim saw the symbol of everything he hated in the world, went into a knife fighter's crouch, while Stone circled to his left. Both focused sharply on each other, and nothing else in the world mattered now. They looked for an opening, a nuance, the telltale sign that betrayed vulnerability, because you only make one mistake in a knife fight: your first, your last, and your only. Stone switched direction, and Ephraim followed him with his eyes, flicking his knife from side to side.

"You runnin' away from me, Massa John. You ain't skeered of a poor nigra, is you?"

"You're always flapping your lips," Stone replied. "Why don't you shut up and fight?"

Ephraim lunged at Stone, and Stone grabbed his knife wrist, while pushing his blade toward Ephraim's belly, but Ephraim clamped his hand around Stone's arm. They were locked together, straining against each other, their faces only inches apart. Stone could see the fury in Ephraim's eyes, and for a moment felt the bear that'd mangled him.

They dug their toes into the dirt and heaved against each other, each trying to press his knife home, but neither would budge. Suddenly Ephraim let go, and stepped to the side. Stone found himself pushing empty air, lost his balance, and fell forward. Ephraim dived forward for the kill, but Stone rolled when he hit the ground and was on his feet in an instant, his blade before him, and Ephraim halted three inches away from its sharpened tip.

Stone circled to his left, holding the blade in front of him. He feinted, but Ephraim punched his blade forward, to cut Stone's arm, and Stone pulled back in time; again no blood was drawn.

Ephraim bent his legs and got lower, and Stone knew he was trying for a belly slash, so he hunkered down too, moving his knife from side to side. Ephraim feinted, and then leapt forward, flashing his knife toward Stone's stomach, but Stone jumped backward, and Ephraim's blade whistled through empty air, while Stone cut down and laid open flesh on Ephraim's shoulder.

An expression of rage came over Ephraim's face as blood showed on his shirt. Stone could see it wasn't a serious wound, but it was first blood, and if he could cut him once, he could cut him again. He switched direction, circling to his right, and Ephraim jumped into his path, blocking his way.

They stared at each other hatefully, then Stone moved to his left, but suddenly Ephraim charged and ripped. Stone raised his arm to protect himself, and Ephraim cut a deep gash on his Stone's forearm, while Stone took a swipe at Ephraim's chest, leaving a long red diagonal line.

Stone felt as if a hot coal had been dropped onto his arm as he stepped back. Ephraim thought Stone was off balance, and rushed forward to stick his knife in, but Stone darted out of the way, and Ephraim found himself facing the open prairie.

Ephraim shifted direction quickly, and Stone wore a cocky half smile. Stone felt certain he could outmaneuver Ephraim, so he feinted to the left, feinted to the right, and then plunged his knife toward Ephraim's heart.

Ephraim's hand snaked up and caught Stone's wrist, while stabbing his knife toward Stone's belly. Stone stopped Ephraim's hand when it was only inches from his stomach, and they were locked together again, straining against each other, gazing into each other's widened eyes, and smelling the coffee on each other's breaths.

Ephraim let up suddenly, hoping Stone would fall on his face, but this time Stone was ready, and cut a three-inch slice out of Ephraim's cheek, while Ephraim slashed Stone's ribs. Both men jumped back, surprised by their sudden wounds, then attacked again, knives flashing in the sunlight. Ephraim whacked a lump off Stone's head, Stone slit Ephraim's bicep, then they caught each other's knife hands and were joined together again in the embrace of death.

They pushed and tugged, but neither was able to achieve an advantage. Ephraim snaked his leg behind Stone and tried to trip him, but Stone bulled forward, and Ephraim lost his balance. He fell to the ground, and Stone landed on top of him, trying to ram his blade into Ephraim's throat, but Ephraim managed to hold his hand back. They rolled across the campsite and came to a stop beside the glowing embers of the fire. Sweat poured from their faces as they grunted and tried to stick in their knives. Ephraim was on the bottom, and Stone on top, when Ephraim heaved like a bucking bronco, and Stone flew backward into the fire pit. He landed on his spine, felt the searing heat, and jumped to his feet as Ephraim rushed toward him, his knife zooming through the air.

All Stone could do to save his life was raise his arm, and Ephraim's blade cut through to the bone. Stone howled in pain and stepped back, while Ephraim rushed forward, back-slashing toward Stone's throat.

Stone ducked and plunged his knife toward Ephraim's belly, but Ephraim's free hand came down and clamped on Stone's wrist, while his knife streaked toward Stone's back. Stone sensed the danger and spun out at the last moment, and Ephraim nearly stabbed himself in the groin.

Both men faced each other in front of the chuck wagon, and both bled from numerous wounds. Their bodies were soaked with sweat, and Stone had lost his hat during the scuffle. Bareheaded, his dark blond hair gleaming in the sunlight, Stone's chest heaved from the exertion.

Ephraim stood before him, face slick with perspiration, as the chuck wagon mules watched solemnly. Then Stone moved to the left, but before he could go three steps, Ephraim screamed and rushed toward him again, stabbing his knife with all his strength toward Stone's heart. Stone dodged out of the way, and the knife rammed into the side of the chuck wagon.

Ephraim pulled the knife, but it wouldn't come loose, and Stone saw his opportunity. He raked his knife across Ephraim's ribs, and Ephraim screamed as he jumped backward. Stone darted between Ephraim and Ephraim's knife, and Ephraim was unarmed, while Stone still held his blade.

A faint smile came over Stone's face, and Ephraim knew he was in deep shit. Stone looked at the knife in his hand, then threw it away disdainfully.

"I'd rather beat you with my fists," he said.

Now they were both unarmed, and raised their hands. Ephraim stepped forward, bobbed and weaved, and threw a left jab at Stone's head, but Stone ducked beneath it and hammered Ephraim in the right kidney, left kidney, and then went upstairs as Ephraim lowered his guard, cracking Ephraim in the nose. Stone kept his fists in constant motion, and moved laterally as Ephraim shot another jab at his head. Stone's head and Ephraim's fist connected, Stone saw a white flash, and then Ephraim punched him in the midsection.

Stone expelled air and doubled over, and Ephraim hit him with an uppercut that straightened him. Stone stumbled backward, fell against the chuck wagon, and Ephraim was all over him, throwing lefts and rights from a variety of angles. Stone ducked and dodged, avoiding most of the punches, but some got through, jolting him. He tried to slide away, but Ephraim kept him pinned against the chuck wagon, hammering him incessantly.

Stone knew he had to launch an attack of his own, otherwise he'd be pummeled into unconsciousness. Ephraim's fists flew so fast they were blurs, but he was overanxious, overextended, and off balance. Stone took one step to the side, simultaneously hurling his fist toward Ephraim's solar plexus. The blow connected, Ephraim's eyes popped out, and his mouth fell open. Stone threw an overhand right that landed on Ephraim's ear, but Ephraim counterpunched Stone's mouth.

Stone's teeth rattled, and he tasted blood on his tongue. Ephraim slammed him in the head three times, then leaned into Stone's sudden sharp uppercut, and went sprawling backward. Stone leapt forward and grabbed Ephraim by the throat. Together they fell to the ground and rolled over, as Stone tried to throttle Ephraim, while Ephraim sought to thumb out Stone's eyes.

They punched, elbowed, kneed, and gouged, and Stone regretted throwing his knife away. Ephraim's hand fell on a length of firewood like a club lying on the ground. He picked it up and bashed Stone's head, and Stone saw stars, wobbled to the side, so Ephraim hit him again, opening a cut on Stone's scalp. Stone dropped to the ground, and Ephraim raised the club in the air. Stone opened his eyes to see it streaking toward his nose, but at the last moment he rolled out. Ephraim leapt forward and smashed him over the head with the club anyway.

Stone saw the white light, and remembered the Gypsy's curse. He raised his arm in time to block another blow, and Ephraim wound up again. The club streaked toward Stone, and Stone caught it in both hands, kicking high with his right foot. The tip of his boot collided with Ephraim's chin, and the impact lifted Ephraim six inches off the ground. Ephraim fell onto his back, and Stone rushed toward him, the club in his hand, to beat him to death. Stone raised the club, aimed it at Ephraim's head, and brought it down with all his strength, but Ephraim scrambled out of the way, and the blow struck him on the buttocks.

Ephraim rose to his feet, spun around, and saw Stone standing with the club in his right hand. The club whistled forward, and Ephraim inadvertently ducked into its path. It broke his nose and sent him flying through the air. He landed on his back, rolled over, and then dived to where he thought Stone's legs would be.

His aim was perfect, he wrapped his arms around Stone's legs, and lurched hard. Stone was flung off his feet, landed in a crunch on his back. Ephraim punched him in the mouth, splitting his lower lip wide open, blood spurting out. Ephraim punched him again, but Stone caught his fist in midair, twisting. Ephraim fell to the side, and Stone dived on him, wrapping his fingers around Ephraim's throat. He pressed his thumbs against Ephraim's Adam's apple, but Ephraim shot both hands through Stone's arms, busting the grip. On their knees, they threw punches at each other, banging each other's head and body. Ephraim saw an opening and delivered a short uppercut to the point of Stone's chin, and Stone's head snapped back. It wasn't the strongest punch Ephraim had thrown, but the accumulation of blows put Stone down.

Stone fell onto his back, his mind was cloudy, and he had to get up, but the ground was undulating beneath him like the deck of a ship at sea. He rolled over and opened his eyes to see a boot steaming toward his face. The boot became larger, blocked out the sun, and crashed into Stone's nose. Stone fell onto his back, and wasn't sure of who he was, but had to get up somehow.

His legs wouldn't work, and a sparrow sang in his ear. He heard a voice above him say: "This is the moment I've waited for all mah life, Massa John."

Seems a shame to kill the man I cured, Ephraim thought as he swung the club at Stone's head, while Stone flashed on an image of Ephraim pissing on his grave. Stone willed himself into sharper focus, and deflected the blow to the side with his arm. Ephraim raised the club for another try, and Stone arose unsteadily to his feet.

The club flew toward Stone's head, and Stone blocked it with another swing of his arm, then dived on Ephraim, who tried to get out of the way at the last moment, but Stone caught his arm and whipped it around. Ephraim went flying through the air, bounced off the chuck wagon, and Stone was all over him immediately, hurling punches before Ephraim could get set. Ephraim managed to duck and block a few, but a straight left jab got through, connecting with Ephraim's forehead and slamming him against the wall of the chuck wagon. Ephraim raised his arms and Stone pounded him in the kidney. Ephraim gasped, and Stone hit him in the same place on his other kidney, and then, when Ephraim lowered his elbows to protect that vital area, Stone punched him squarely in the mouth.

Ephraim collapsed onto his hands and knees. Stone looked around for something to kill him with, saw the poker, and picked it up, raised it, and sent it crashing toward Ephraim's head. Ephraim heard the whistle of iron, and something told him to dodge. He lurched to the side and the poker struck a rock on the ground, sparks flying through the air. Stone turned and prepared for another blow, when Ephraim spotted a rock the size of a fist on the ground. Swooping down, he snatched it in his hand and threw it at Stone's head.

Stone raised his arm to protect himself, and Ephraim tackled him, knocking him to the ground. *What a waste of a beautiful day,* Stone thought as he let go of the poker and tried to ram his thumbs into Ephraim's eyes. Ephraim grabbed Stone's wrists and bucked hard, causing Stone to lose his balance. Stone fell to the side, they broke apart; both scrambled to their feet.

Stone charged first, and Ephraim timed him coming in. Stone was off balance, too eager, and wide open. Ephraim launched a terrific right jab to Stone's head, and it was like the collision of two freight trains.

Stone was dazed, but swung viciously at Ephraim, who slipped the punch easily and nailed Stone with a hook to the kidney Stone grunted, and shot a left jab to Ephraim's eye, opening a cut on the lid. Ephraim replied with a right cross to Stone's cheek, a left hook to his nose, and an uppercut to the tip of his chin, but Stone leaned back and countered with a jab that pulped Ephraim's mouth, and a right cross that spun his head around. Ephraim felt like he was dragging a bale of cotton behind him, and it was his own body.

They stood toe to toe and battered each other, and neither stepped backward an inch. All strategy and tactics were gone as they tried to beat each other into submission. Each landed crushing blows on the other, but nobody went down. *Jesus Christ, I'm in it again,* Stone thought. *What's wrong with me?*

If he fell, he'd knew he'd never get up again. Somehow he had to stay on his feet and destroy Ephraim, but so far Ephraim had taken his best shots and didn't go down. Stone dug in his heels and threw devastating punches at Ephraim's face, a mask of blood in front of him, while absorbing terrific punches to his own body and face. The winner would be the man who could stay on his feet and keep punching no matter what.

On cliffs in distant mountains, lobos watched with keen eyes. It looked like another easy meal. *They do our work for us.*

Stone's arms were leaden, his breath came in gasps, and he swallowed blood from his shattered lips. His left eye was half-closed and his right ear was nearly torn off, but he could see Ephraim was bloody from head to toe, and Ephraim's nose had been flattened.

It occurred to Stone that they were killing each other, but it was satisfying to beat the man you hated most in the world, a man who'd insulted you beyond redemption. Stone didn't care if he died, as long as he killed Ephraim. Stone threw a weary arm punch at Ephraim, and Ephraim flung one back. Their strength had been sapped, and they couldn't hurt each other anymore, but still they staggered from side to side and threw fists at each other. Stone knew he had to pull a good one up from someplace, and Ephraim reached the same conclusion. Both of them sucked up their remaining reserves of strength, took aim, and launched their fists at each other's heads. They connected simultaneously, and both fell on their asses. Stone spat blood as he struggled to get up, when he became aware of a faint yipping sound in the air, like dogs barking.

He turned in the direction of the sound and saw an immense Indian war party charging toward him out of the distant hills. This is what happens when you're not vigilant, goddammit... Ephraim dived on him, and Stone wasn't sure he'd really seen what his eyeballs just showed him, but he heard the war whoops again, and Ephraim stiffened.

Ephraim spun his head around, and both looked at Indians galloping toward them, shaking their war lances and bows, making a ululating sound with their mouths. They jumped to their feet, and Stone saw his knife lying on the ground. He picked it up and ran toward Tomahawk, who was gazing at the Indians with alarm. Ephraim meanwhile untied his horse from the back of the chuck wagon, leapt into the saddle and was off.

Stone spurred Tomahawk, and the animal threw himself into a gallop, as an arrow whistled over Stone's head. Stone looked over his shoulder and saw Indians swarming over the prairie, screaming and shaking their weapons. He pulled out his gun and fired two warning shots, then looked at Ephraim twenty yards away and thought of blowing him out of the saddle, but that wasn't a good idea strategically, because they'd need every rifle they had to hold off the Indians.

Stone had never been taken unawares during the war. He'd posted sentries and always kept his senses alert for Yankees, but now he'd been fighting with the goddamn cook, of all people, in what was essentially enemy territory. *I was a sharp young cavalry officer, and Wade Hampton himself asked for my opinions at staff meetings, but now I'm just another brawling cowboy. West Point officers don't get into fistfights with the cook, especially when the enemy can strike at any moment.*

Tomahawk galloped over the top of a rise, and Stone saw the herd in the distance. He turned in his saddle, took aim, and fired into the mass of Indians. One of them let go of his reins, slid down the side of his horse, and fell beneath the horse's hooves. Stone fired again, but the bullet kicked up dirt next to the front entrance of a prairie dog den.

In the den, falling clods of earth fell on the head of the hapless prairie dog. *There they go again,* he thought, hearing hoofbeats pass over him, as more dirt dropped to the tunnel floor.

The Indians rushed over the rise, pursuing Stone and Ephraim, and Ephraim drew his pistol, aimed at the Indians, and pulled the trigger. His gun fired, one Indian fell off his horse, but the others kept charging relentlessly, screaming and yelling battle cries. Stone looked ahead and saw cowboys riding toward the drag, while the herd already was in full stampede, fleeing from the gunfire and Indians. Nearly three thousand cattle spread out like a massive blot, covering an enormous acreage, while cowboys set up a defense where the drag had been.

Stone and Ephraim raced over the grass, with the Indians hot on their heels. Stone was in the lead, and now Truscott and the others were only a few hundred yards away. Turning in his saddle, Stone fired a shot at the Indians as a hail of arrows flew around him. The Indians' legs flopped up and down as they shook their weapons, their faces mad with fury. Tomahawk's hoofbeats thundered on the ground as he charged toward the cowboys. Stone could make out Truscott, Don Emilio, and Cassandra with a face white as snow, but her rifle was ready for war. Truscott and the cowboys had shot their horses, to make a barricade of their dead flesh.

Tomahawk leapt over them, landing among the cowboys. Stone jumped down from the saddle, and Tomahawk kept running, because he didn't want to become anybody's barricade. A few moments later Ephraim's horse jumped behind the barricades, but Ephraim shot him through the head before he could get away. The animal fell in a clump to the ground, and Ephraim dropped on his belly behind him, opening fire on the charging Indians.

Arrows slammed into the ground all around the cowboys as they sighted down their barrels at the onrushing Indians. Stone leapt behind Cassandra's horse and looked at her, but she was steady, squeezing the trigger of her rifle. It fired, kicked into her shoulder, and in the distance an Indian warrior dropped off his saddle.

Stone raised his rifle and took aim at the lead Indian, who was hollering at the top of his lungs and swinging his war club in the air. Stone squeezed off the round, the rifle fired, and the Indian fell backward over the rump of his war pony.

The other Indians charged onward, firing arrows at the cowboys who send forth a barrage of gunfire. Indians fell from their horses, but the rest continued their attack, yelling and urging each other on. They were fifty yards away now, and the cowboys were greatly outnumbered, but the cowboys had modern rifles, while most of the Indians carried stone-age weapons. Cassandra drew a bead on the leader, an old man wearing a warbonnet made of white feathers, and shot him out of his saddle.

The Indians were almost on top of them now, and Stone grabbed Cassandra's wrist. "Save a bullet for yourself!" he told her, and then turned to meet the shrieking band of Indians.

A horse leapt up in front of Stone, and Stone shot the animal in the belly. The horse whinnied as it flew over Stone's head, hit the ground, and didn't get up, but its rider was thrown clear. Stone turned around in time to see a war hatchet zooming toward his head, and he ducked at the last moment. The war hatchet passed over his head, and Stone arose, firing his rifle from the hip at the Indian; a red dot appeared on the Indian's chest.

Stone didn't have time to see the Indian fall, because he heard an Indian running toward him, a war lance in his hand. Stone raised the rifle and fired.

Click!

In all the world, from heaven to hell, from the dust of the prairie to the fire of the sun, there was no more mournful sound. The rifle was empty, and the Indian thrust the spear toward Stone's chest. Stone parried the lance with his rifle, and slammed the rifle butt into the Indian's skull. There was a sickening thunk, and the Indian's eyes rolled into his head. He fell to the ground, but behind him were two more Indians, one carrying a lance, the other a war hatchet, and both screamed horribly as they rushed toward Stone.

He held his rifle like a club and swung with both hands at the Indian carrying the hatchet as the Indian slammed his hatchet's blade into Stone's rifle. Steel struck steel, sparks flew into the air, and the Indian lost his grip on the hatchet. Stone plucked it out of the air as the other Indian pushed his war lance toward Stone's ribs. Stone batted it out of the way with his forearm, and buried the hatchet in the Indian's head. Blood and brains flew in all directions, and Stone swung around, slamming the hatchet into the jaw of the next Indian, severing it from his face. Stone jumped over the Indian, and landed in front of another Indian with a rusty old gun in his hand.

Stone ducked, and the bullet rocketed through the air over his head. One of Stone's hands wrapped around the hot barrel of the gun, and his other hand gripped the Indian's throat. Stone squeezed, trying to throttle the Indian, while the Indian struggled and tried to kick Stone in the groin.

Stone dodged the Indian's kicks, but the Indian broke out of his grasp. Stone dived for the Indian's gun again, and the Indian raised it for a shot. Stone grabbed the gun, it fired, and a bullet zipped into the sky. The Indian fell backward, and Stone landed on top of him.

They rolled around on the grass, fighting for possession of the gun. The Indian reached to his belt and yanked out a knife with a six-inch blade, and Stone grasped his wrist. The Indian kicked and bucked, they tossed about, and Stone rode him like a wild mustang. It was like fighting a strange foreign creature whose musculature had a different tension, wild and slippery, utterly lethal. The Indian spit in Stone's face, and Stone let go of the Indian's knife hand, pounding him in the face with all his strength.

The Indian was stunned, and Stone took the gun from his hand, turned it around, and shot the Indian in a main artery of his chest. Blood spurted out, and Stone jumped up in time to confuse the aim of another Indian who'd been aiming an arrow at him.

The arrow hissed through the air past Stone's ear, and Stone raised the gun, took quick aim, and fired. The gun kicked in his hand, and the Indian showed an astonished expression. *A white man who's one with his weapon has killed me.* Then the Indian's knees crumpled and he collapsed onto the ground.

Stone flashed on Cassandra, and turned toward where she'd been, but an Indian was there, thrusting his war lance at Stone's chest. Stone darted to the side and fired the gun, and the Indian was knocked to the ground, blood dripping from a hole in his stomach.

Fighting raged around Stone as he glanced at the gun, an old Whitneyville-Hartford Dragoon, stolen from some bullwhacker, long dead. Then he remembered Cassandra again, and turned in her direction. She crouched on the ground, Colt in hand, and in front of her lay four dead Indians, while two live ones rushed her, brandishing hatchets. Stone shouted and ran toward them, firing the Whitneyville-Hartford, while Cassandra shot from her position. The Indians were caught in a murderous crossfire, and spun through the air, blood spiraling from their wounds.

Stone moved toward Cassandra, and she swung the gun at him, then realized who he was. He landed beside her, looked her over, and turned around, expecting to see a horde of Indians charging, but instead the Indians were retreating! The defensive perimeter was covered with smoke and dust as the Indians ran back to their horses.

"Hold yer fire!" Truscott shouted.

There was silence, and then Roberto said weakly, "I theenk I am going to die." He lay on the ground, a war lance sticking out of his chest, pinning him to the dirt. "The son om a beetch got me," he said as blood burbled out of his mouth. "Is Don Emilio there?"

"Estoy aqui, amigo."

Roberto looked up at Don Emilio and said, "Shoot me."

Don Emilio aimed his gun at Roberto's head, and Cassandra turned away. The gun fired.

"Anybody else hurt?" asked Truscott.

"They got Joe Little Bear," Duvall replied.

At Duvall's feet lay Joe Little Bear, stripped naked, blood on his chest, a strip of hair gone from the top of his head, and his genitals stuffed into his throat, the punishment for a traitor.

"Anybody else!" Truscott hollered.

Nobody said anything.

"Load yer guns! They'll be back!"

Stone's cartridges couldn't be used in the Whitneyville-Hartford Dragoon. He stuffed it into his belt and searched for the Colt he'd dropped early in the fight.

"Comanches," Slipchuck said, thumbing bullets into the magazine of his Henry. "Worst goddamn savages you could hope for, except maybe the Apache."

Stone found his Colt next to the bodies of dead Comanches. It felt better in his hand than the Whitneyville-Hartford, and he had enough ammunition to put up a respectable fight. Then he found his rifle, but Tomahawk had run off with the saddlebags containing his extra ammunition.

Stone returned to Cassandra, who was plundering her own saddlebags. Her cowboy hat was perched on her head, a crazed gleam was in her eye, and he knew she'd never be the same, if she survived today. She looked at him, and became aware for the first time of his bloody, banged-up face, but assumed the Indians had done it. "What happened?"

"Injuns attacked while we were breaking camp."

Stone looked for Ephraim, and saw him on the other side of the barricade, his face mangled, a rifle in his hand. Ephraim glanced at Stone, and they turned away from each other. Stone looked in the direction the Indians had gone, and thought he and the others probably would be wiped out within the hour.

"Unnh!" said the *segundo*, walking toward Truscott and holding out his gun. "Unnh!"

Truscott handed him a box of cartridges, and the *segundo* walked off stiffly, his face a lump of clay. The other men lay behind their dead horses, and faced the direction the Indians had gone. A breeze whistled among the blades of grass, and a few wispy clouds floated past the bright blue sky.

"When they come," Truscott said, "give 'em lead! It's the only thing they respect!"

Stone thought they didn't have a chance, because there were too many Comanches, and not enough cowboys and vaqueros with rifles. They'd simply be overwhelmed, but they'd take Comanches with them.

Cassandra looked at John Stone. "I guess this is it," she said, a lump in her throat.

"Afraid so," he replied.

Her face was streaked with sweat, but her beautiful eyes shone through. "You know," she said, "if things'd been different, we might've . . ."

Her voice trailed off. They looked at each other, and realized they'd die side by side.

"Yes, it's too bad," he muttered.

"If there's one thing I regret," Slipchuck said ruefully, "it's I never been to Frisco. Drove stagecoaches all over, but never made it to the one place I always wanted to go. They say they got the best whorehouses in the world."

Truscott spit tobacco juice at the ground as he sat on his dead horse's rump. "They have, but you got to pay for it, and it don't come cheap. Then when you're finished, on yer way home, you got to watch out somebody don't come up behind you and hit you over the head with a billy."

"Prob'ly," agreed Slipchuck philosophically, "but jest once in me life I'd like ter have a fancy whore. What do they do that costs so much, Ramrod? You ever take one on?"

"A few times," said Truscott, old whoremaster from way back. "They're usually prettier than yer average saloon whore, and they got ladylike manners like Cassandra here, but when you take off their clothes, it's all pretty much the same. I remember once in Frisco I . . ."

Cassandra listened raptly, while trying to appear nonchalant. Indians were going to massacre them, and they were spending their final moments discussing their favorite infamous subject. It was amazing, their dedication to that subject.

"We went up to her room," Truscott continued, the old raconteur, "and she says, 'What do you want?' I says, 'Everything you got.' She says, 'You ain't got that much money.' I says, 'Oh, yes I have,' and throw fifty dollars on the bed. She counts it, and her eyes look like goose eggs. 'You got it,' she said to me. 'Take off yer clothes.'"

"Where'd you get the fifty dollars?" Slipchuck asked.

Duvall smacked Slipchuck hard on the shoulder. "Who cares where he got the fifty dollars? I wanna hear about the whore. Shut yer fuckin' mouth."

"I did like she told me," Truscott said, without breaking his rhythm, "and got onto the bed, a big brass four-poster with a mirror on the ceiling."

"A mirror on the ceiling?" Moose Roykins asked, an awed smile on his face, imagining the possibilities.

"Mirrors on the walls too. Mirrors everywhere, and a crystal chandelier. It was the top floor of the Versailles Hotel. All the big politicians and lawyers used to stop there. The governor might've been right down the hall while I was there, for all I know."

"To hell with the governor!" Duvall expostulated. "Who cares about the fuckin' governor? Tell me about the whore!"

"I didn't even say what she looked like," Truscott said, whetting their appetites. "She had black hair, and was built like a brick shithouse, with every brick in place. She'd make Cassandra here look like a little boy, if you know what I mean. Then she took off her clothes, and got onto the bed with me. Now at the time I thought I'd seen and done it all, and I been in every whoop and holler from the Mississippi to the Pacific, but this whore had a trick that even I'd never seen, and I . . ."

One moment the prairie was still, and then suddenly Comanches appeared over the nearby hills, shrieking wildly, charging toward the cowboys! Cassandra and her men stared at them, switching gears from Truscott's narrative, the whore completely forgotten as they dived to the ground.

"Don't fire till I give the word!" Truscott said.

Everyone got ready, aiming his or her rifle, while Comanches raced toward them, screaming and yelling, waving weapons in the air. Stone could see with his professional cavalry officer's eyes that they were hugely outnumbered, the Indian attack was focused and coordinated, and it would certainly wipe them out. He looked at Cassandra, and her face was in repose as she held her rifle steady and sighted down the barrel. She appeared resigned to death, and a tremendous affection for her came over him when he realized she'd go down like a soldier.

He wanted to say something tender, but there wasn't time. The warriors galloped toward them, sliding up and down the sides of their horses, even passing underneath their horses' bellies. Wind rustled their ornate warbonnets and their horses' manes as they charged closer. Stone aimed his sights at one of the leaders, and waited for Truscott to give the order. In moments the massacre would begin, but he'd save his last bullet for a Comanche, and when he ran out of bullets, he had his old Apache knife stained with Ephraim's blood.

Arrows whizzed over his head, but he didn't dare duck because firepower was the only weapon they had, and every shot had to count. The end, when it came, would be swift and bloody. He sighted down the barrel of his rifle, and at its end, behind bead curtains, the Gypsy hag threw down the ace of spades.

"Unnh!" the *segundo* bellowed.

Everyone looked toward him, and he was on his feet, rifle in hand, walking woodenly toward the barricade. He climbed over the horses and marched toward the charging Comanches.

"Git back here!" Truscott hollered.

The *segundo* didn't respond, and continued his advance toward the Comanches. Everyone was sure the Comanches would shoot him down and trample him into the dirt, ride right over him, and keep going.

Like a monster from a cave, the *segundo* walked rigidly toward the Indians, and the young warriors headed for him, aiming rifles, arrows, and war lances. They let fly their arrows, and bullets whizzed like angry gnats, but the *segundo* didn't falter. He continued his lone harrowing trek toward them, and they raced closer, firing pistols and arrows. One warrior dashed in boldly, whacked the *segundo*'s head with his hatchet, but the hatchet bounced off the *segundo*'s skull, and the *segundo* continued walking, making his weird nasal sound. "Unnh! Unnh!"

The charge broke apart around the *segundo*. Somehow the Indians couldn't kill him, and they pulled back their reins, eyeing him curiously. War ponies danced about excitedly as the warriors shouted at each other.

The *segundo* stopped and raised his arms, shaking them mightily in the air. "Unnh!"

The Comanches shrieked in terror, turned their ponies around, and galloped away. The cowboys watched in amazement as the Comanches fled in disarray toward the hills, while the *segundo* stood triumphantly in the middle of the prairie, bellowing nasally and shaking his fists in the air.

10

IT TOOK THE rest of the day to round up the horses and locate the main herd. The longhorns munched grass and looked up lazily as the cowboys approached. Cassandra had been around cattle long enough to make an approximate count, and she figured a thousand were missing, scattered all over the region. It'd take days to round them up, if the Comanches left them alone.

"Might as well make camp right here," Truscott said.

They unsaddled their horses and turned them loose to graze, while the herd rumbled and mooed. The cowboys gathered wood for a fire, and at sunset Ephraim returned with two vaqueros.

"Injuns burned the chuck wagon," Ephraim said. "Stoled everythin' worth stealin'."

Everybody groaned, because they knew it meant nothing but beef until the next town, if they made it to the next town. Ephraim returned with a steer and butchered it methodically, with no special flourishes. He chopped off chunks of meat and parceled them to the men, who stuck the meat on the ends of sticks, and held the sticks over the fire. Life would be primitive until they could buy more kitchen utensils.

The campsite filled with the fragrance of roasting meat, and the sun sank behind the vast plain to the left, silhouetted by a blood-red sky. Globules of fat dripped into the fire, and Stone looked at Ephraim through the flames. They hadn't spoken since the fight, and neither had suggested they go off to finish what they'd started. Stone wasn't anxious to tangle with Ephraim again, and Ephraim evidently felt the same way.

The cowboys pulled the meat from the fire and lay it on the grass, attacking it with their knives, and if it wasn't done enough, they put it back over the flames. Meat and water for dinner, but it was better than eating a goddamned lizard.

"Injuns won't be back," Truscott said.

"What makes you think so?" Cassandra asked.

"They was scared shitless." He looked at the *segundo*, gnawing a bone like a dog. "And I don't blame 'em."

Cassandra turned to the *segundo*. What would they do with him when they reached Abilene? The people might not understand, and Cassandra wasn't even sure *she* understood.

"Hey, Ramrod," Slipchuck said, the thread of his thought unbroken, "why don't you tell us the end of that story?"

"What story?" as if he didn't know.

"The one about the whore in the fancy cathouse in San Francisco."

"Oh, that whore. Where was I?"

"You was in bed with her, and she had this great trick you was gonna tell us. What was it?"

"Wa'al," Truscott explained clinically, "I got on the bottom, and she got on the top, and she kind of . . ."

Cassandra cleared her throat. "Excuse me, but I think we ought to raise ourselves from the muck into which this conversation has fallen. May I suggest we get down on our knees, and thank God for His assistance and love?"

The men groaned, because they'd rather hear the story of the whore. Truscott turned to Cassandra and said, "These men fought off a Comanche war party today, and if they want to talk about whores, I believe it's their right."

Cassandra couldn't argue with the inexorable truth of that statement, but she didn't want to listen to their whorehouse banter. She arose to leave, when suddenly Ben Thorpe stopped eating. "I heard something," he said.

They reached for their guns. The sound of hoofbeats came to them through the night, and it sounded like a large number of horses walking slowly.

"They're headed this way," Truscott said. "We better git set."

Once more the story of the whorehouse was forgotten as they arranged their saddles in a line facing the oncoming riders, and then took cover. Holding rifles ready to fire, they listened to approaching hoofbeats, and it sounded like a procession instead of a full-tilt Comanche attack.

"Might be the cavalry," Moose Roykins said hopefully.

"Cavalry makes more noise than that," Slipchuck replied. "Soldiers carry too much junk."

"Can't understand it," Truscott said. "Injuns generally don't attack at night."

The cowboys, vaqueros, and Cassandra got ready, and everyone expected a hand-to-hand battle with naked savages in the dark. The *segundo* sat cross-legged behind his saddle, his back straight, staring at the sounds and muttering "Unnh" quietly to himself.

Comanches came into view out of the night, a long line of riders wearing ceremonial dress but no war paint. They stopped, and then two young warriors rode forward, each carrying the white flag of truce, while behind them rode an older warrior wearing an elaborate warbonnet.

"They want to powwow," Truscott said, "but it's a trick, if I know injuns. Git ready to fire."

"Wait a minute—don't anybody fire!" Cassandra countermanded him. "Let's see what they want!"

Truscott turned to her. "They'll stake you on an anthill, after they pass you around the tribe."

"Better talk than fight, but if I have to fight, I will!"

Cassandra rose to her feet, and Stone stood beside her. The *segundo* lumbered drunkenly to her other side, and then Truscott joined them. Together they waited for the three Comanches to come closer. If it were only cattle they wanted, Cassandra'd give it to them. Anything was better than dead men.

The Comanches drew closer, and the two young ones pulled their horses to the side, making way for the older warrior behind them who raised his arm and showed his open palm. "How, John!" he said.

Truscott raised his own empty hand. "How!"

The Comanche sat proudly on his saddle, his hair hanging to his shoulders, and the front of his warbonnet decorated with silver disks. He cleared his throat and spoke slowly. "You have great medicine man . . . with you. Our medicine man . . . want powwow with him."

The cowboys looked at each other in confusion for a few moments, then slowly turned to Ephraim, who was raising himself to his full height, a strange glint in his eyes. "Tell your medicine man we can powwow whenever he want."

The warrior turned around and shouted something, then three other warriors detached themselves from the main body of Comanches and moved forward. The warriors on the outside were young, but the one in the middle was a wizened old man with skin the color of parchment, his ribs showing through his skin, wearing a ceremonial warbonnet with two buffalo horns sticking out. He wore numerous necklaces of beads and stones, a silver bracelet encircled his wrist, and he held a dried hawk in his right hand.

"This is Iron Pants," the spokesman said.

Iron Pants climbed down from his horse, stood before Ephraim, and touched his fist to Ephraim's heart. "Come."

Iron Pants walked toward the prairie, and Ephraim hesitated for only a moment before following him. Everyone watched them go, and soon the night swallowed them up. The Comanches climbed down from their horses and sat cross-legged upon the ground, while Stone watched them warily.

Truscott stared in the direction Ephraim had gone with Iron Pants. "Wonder what that's all about?" he said, scratching the back of his head.

"You were all set to fight," Cassandra told him, "and if we listened to you, we'd be dead."

"It ain't over yet."

"At least we're still alive."

Truscott took off his hat and threw it on the ground. "If I ever sign on another cattle drive with a goddamn woman, I hope God reaches out of the sky, grabs me by the hair, and dumps my head in horseshit!"

"You smell as if God did that three weeks ago," Cassandra said. "You're just a crotchety old polecat who always has to have his own way."

Cassandra turned up her nose and walked away, while Truscott sputtered into his mustache. Several minutes passed, and Ephraim didn't return. The cowboys sat around their campfire, cleaning and loading guns, casting glances at the Comanches encamped nearby.

Truscott lit a cigarette. "Maybe they killed him," he said.

"Don't think they'd dare," Slipchuck replied. "They're skeered of him, and to tell you the truth, so'm I."

Cassandra sat near Stone, who smoked a cigarette and looked in the direction Ephraim had gone with the Comanche medicine man. The breeze picked up, and the sky filled with clouds. The cowboys threw more logs on the flames, and the Comanches drifted toward the campfire, sat down with the cowboys and vaqueros, who were tense and defensive, expecting an attack at any moment, but the Comanches appeared friendly. The Comanches asked for tobacco, and the cowboys gave it to them. The atmosphere became relaxed, the prairie was silent, and Slipchuck saw his chance.

"Hey, Ramrod," he said, "you ain't finished the story about the whore."

Truscott looked at him blankly. "What whore was that?"

"The one in the fancy whorehouse in Frisco, who had the special trick. What was it?"

"Oh, that," Truscott said, and then spit a lunger into the fire. "Well, she . . ."

Cassandra cleared her throat. "I'm sorry, but I don't like this story. Tell it when you get to Abilene, when I'm not around, if you don't mind."

Duvall slapped her leg. "Aw, don't be a pain in the ass, Cassandra. It's a good story, and all of us might learn something, even you."

"I'm sure it's something we all can do without. We should direct our attention to the finer things."

Slipchuck replied, "They say the finest whorehouses in the world are in San Francisco. If that's not fine, then what the hell's fine?"

She sighed in exasperation. Nothing could be done with them. They were just a bunch of billygoats. Meanwhile, a burly Comanche warrior plopped himself down beside Truscott. "I give you three horses for the woman," he said, pointing at Cassandra.

"She ain't worth three horses," Truscott said gruffly.

"How many horses you take?"

"She's ain't for sale, but by Christ I wish she were."

The Indian arose and walked toward Cassandra, looking down at her. "He your man?" the Indian asked, pointing to Stone.

"No."

The Indian turned to Stone. "I fight you for her."

"She's not mine."

The Comanche appeared confused, then grabbed Cassandra's arm roughly. "If the old man not your father, and you not belong this man, you belong me." He yanked her to her feet.

"Get your hands off me," Cassandra replied in a deadly tone, pointing her Colt at his nose.

The Comanche blinked in astonishment as Cassandra drew back the hammer with her thumb. Another Comanche shouted, and the warrior let Cassandra go. Grumbling something unintelligible, the warrior walked away from the fire as the other Comanches laughed.

Cassandra returned to her seat on the ground, and looked at the Comanches. For a moment she'd thought the party was over, but the Comanches appeared calm and jovial, and there was something free about them, whereas her cowboys and vaqueros were edgy, and never let their hands roam far from their guns.

Nobody dared sleep with Comanches in the vicinity. But the Comanches didn't seem tired. A group of them chanted near the campfire, while others casually wandered into a circle and danced. At first their movements were lazy, but gradually became more lively as they jumped around first on one foot and then the other.

"Hey . . . hey . . . hey . . . hey . . ."

They chanted into the night, and Cassandra thought how strange it was to be alone in the middle of a vast wilderness, with Indians dancing around a fire. Some Indians on the sidelines tapped sticks together, and one made an eerie whistle like a hawk descending on his prey. The fire projected flames onto their bodies, and they looked as though they were dancing in hell.

"Hey . . . hey . . . hey . . . hey . . ."

A Comanche leaned toward Stone and held out his hand. "Come—dance."

Stone rose to his feet and followed the Indian toward the circle of dancing warriors, while other Comanches led cowboys and vaqueros toward the dancers. Soon all of the cowboys were jumping in a big circle around the bonfire, while a few Comanches beat sticks and chanted in the center.

A Comanche warrior with a hatchet in his belt walked toward Cassandra. "You too."

"Oh, no," she replied. "I don't dance. It's just for men, isn't it?"

"For all warriors. You are warrior too. You must dance."

He took her hand and pulled her toward the fire, and it lighted tiny emeralds in her eyes. She moved into the circle and hopped first on one foot and then the other, like the rest of them. Then she clapped her hands and joined their chant.

"Hey . . . hey . . . hey . . . hey . . ."

Stone wagged his arms and danced around the circle, studying the Indians, trying to understand them. During the day they'd cut off your private parts and stuff them into your mouth, and at night they danced with you. Indians, Mexicans, and Americans wiggled around the fire, under the constellation of Orion the Warrior.

The dance continued into the night, and the fire blazed brightly, illuminating the strange scene, casting elongated shadows upon the ground. Occasionally someone threw another log on the fire, and the sparks flared up. The repetitive chanting and dancing drew Stone into a mild hypnotic trance, but the Comanches appeared happy, and he figured a happy Comanche was probably not a dangerous Comanche.

A cheer went up among the Comanches, and all of them looked toward the prairie, where Ephraim and Iron Pants were emerging from the darkness side by side, and Ephraim carried a small leather pouch in his hand.

"Hey . . . hey . . . hey . . . hey . . ."

The Comanches made a path for them, and Iron Pants and Ephraim walked side by side toward the fire, their eyes glassy. They stopped near the bright flames, faced each other, and touched each other's hearts with their fists.

Then Iron Pants turned to the nearest Comanche, who shouted an order. A different Comanche appeared with a horse, and Iron Pants climbed into the saddle. He rode away from the fire, with the warriors behind him, a long procession leading into the darkness. Cassandra and the cowboys watched them disappear, and then only their faint receding voices could be heard.

"Hey . . . hey . . . hey . . . hey . . ."

Cassandra and the cowboys were alone by the fire, and everyone's attention turned to Ephraim, who'd dropped to a cross-legged seating position, staring fixedly at the dancing flames, as if they contained the truth of the universe. Everyone wanted to know what happened, but were afraid to ask. They remembered the *segundo*, the cure of John Stone, and now the Comanches. Who was this Ephraim?

Stone stared at him, chilled deep in his bones, because Ephraim knew things he'd never dreamed of. It wasn't healthy to have an enemy like Ephraim.

"You all right, cookie?" Truscott asked.

Ephraim didn't respond for several seconds as he continued gazing through half-closed eyes at the fire. "I'm all right," he said at last.

"Injuns gone for good, you think?"

"Yes."

"What's in the bag?"

Ephraim sat still, and the wind blew a gust that made the fire crackle and grow hotter. A log exploded, showering sparks into the air.

Ephraim turned his head toward Truscott, and then his eyes roved over the faces of every cowboy and vaquero in the outfit. He picked up the leather bag at his feet, tipped it upside down, and its contents fell out.

They expected trinkets, the head of a dead hawk, or maybe a magical Comanche amulet, but instead small, roundish, dark-colored objects fell to the ground, and it looked like bark or other vegetative matter.

"What is it?" Truscott asked, kneeling beside Ephraim. He picked one up, turned it over in his fingers, and sniffed it. "What does it do?"

Ephraim put one into his mouth and chewed as he stared into the fire.

"It's somethin' to eat," Truscott said, raising it to his lips.

A bony hand appeared out of the night and grabbed Truscott's wrist. "Wouldn't do that if I were you, Ramrod," said Slipchuck.

"Why in hell not?"

"Might be pizzoned."

Truscott chinned toward Ephraim. "Ain't killed him." He held the stuff out to Don Emilio. "You ever see this before?"

Don Emilio gazed at it. "Never," he replied.

Ephraim spoke, and his voice was even lower than his usual baritone. "It grow out here. Iron Pants say it the medicine of the Great Spirit."

"Iron Pants eat any?"

"Yep."

Truscott bit a tiny bit off with his tobacco-stained teeth, and chewed it. "Tastes bitter."

Ephraim looked up at him. "Make you drunk, like whiskey," he said, flames dancing like dragons across his eyeballs.

"Whiskey?" Truscott raised the medicine to his mouth, and Slipchuck held his wrist again. "You said it yourself, Ramrod. Never put somethin' in yer mouth, you don't know what it is."

"He's right," Cassandra said. "We need to keep our wits about us."

"You keep your wits about yerself, if that's what you want, Mrs. Whiteside," Truscott replied, "but I been drinkin' whiskey when you was just a gleam in yer daddy's eye. Last time I was in San Antone, I drank three bottles of the worst rotgut the world ever saw, and broke one bottle over the sheriff's head, so what's this damned dried cowshit gonna do to me?" He stuffed the medicine into his mouth and chewed defiantly. "If it's anythin' like whiskey, I can use it!"

The other cowboys stared at Truscott as he picked up another piece of medicine and put it into his mouth. Then the cowboys turned to Ephraim, who smiled faintly as he stared into the fire. Truscott munched his third chunk of medicine, one eye raised skeptically.

"Don't feel nothin'," he muttered.

The cowboys picked up medicine, and Stone was among them, wanting his share. He placed a handful in his mouth, and they had an odd tangy taste like an orange peel left in the sun too long.

Cassandra watched the cowboys and vaqueros gobble the gift from the Comanche medicine man. She didn't want a crew of drunken crazy cowboys, and she the only woman around. Released from their ordinary restraints, they might do anything, but she couldn't simply leave. The prairie was full of Comanches who'd treat her even worse than cowboys. She'd have to stay at the campsite and defend herself, and if they came for her, maybe a few well-placed bullets would stop them.

She watched the cowboys warily as they sat on the ground in a circle around the fire, and they stared at it like Ephraim. Who were these men, who one moment could be engrossed in the most sordid degraded episode of prostitution she'd ever heard, and the next moment look like statues of the Buddha she'd seen once in an illustrated cultural magazine printed in New York City. A half hour passed, and then they crawled or staggered to their blankets, collapsed onto the ground, and fell asleep.

Cassandra couldn't drift off, although she was bone-tired. She'd fought an Indian battle, it hadn't been her average day, and her mind was alive with images of Indians trying to kill her. And then there'd been the incredible story of the whorehouse in San Francisco. Cassandra actually was curious about the prostitute's special technique, because she sincerely wanted to be a good wife in every way if she ever got married again, although it appeared unlikely, because she was losing her beauty in the hot, dry prairie air.

Cowboys and vaqueros snored around her, and the fire died down. Unable to rest, she arose and looked at them, and all were motionless except the *segundo*, who sat with a rifle cradled in his lap, searching with his little pig eyes, listening for signs of danger. He and Cassandra were the only ones who hadn't touched the medicine lying on the ground at Ephraim's feet.

The Negro cook lay on his back, a beatific smile on his face. Cassandra turned toward the remuda, where the night horses were saddled and ready to ride. Her men slumbered peacefully, and a few snored. She wondered if she should try some of the medicine too, to help her sleep.

It lay in a heap beside Ephraim, and she knelt beside him, picking one up. It obviously was part of a plant, and looked like a dried slice of sausage. She placed it like a sacrament onto her tongue, and it was hard as a rock. The others had eaten three or four, so she sat by the smoldering embers of the fire and chewed them down. Then she returned to her blankets, drank from her canteen, and lay down.

She felt vague warmth radiating out from her spine, and it was cozy to be wrapped in her blankets. The day had been murderous, but now all anxiety evaporated from her mind. She was safe, everything would be all right, and all she needed was sleep.

She closed her eyes, and breathed deeply, as the *segundo* gazed vacantly into the moonless night.

11

STONE WAS AWAKENED by tiny bells tinkling in the distance. He opened his eyes and saw spiderweb patterns of green and red against the dark night sky. His body tingled as he raised himself to a sitting position.

Some of the others stumbled about drunkenly. One of the vaqueros squeezed a handful of dirt and giggled like a child. Ephraim chanted unintelligibly, a gold chain in his hand.

Stone thought he was dreaming. Everything was so peculiar, and the bells continued to peal in his ear. He felt like laughing, or maybe crying, and wanted to be alone, away from the others. He had the presence of mind to make certain his gun was in its holster, and then plucked his old Confederate cavalry hat off the pommel of his saddle. He pulled the hat squarely onto his head and roamed off onto the open prairie.

He knew there were Comanches in the area, but he'd sat around the campfire with them, and they were friends now. Iron Pants had given them the medicine of the Great Spirit—what could go wrong? He walked from the campsite and climbed to the top of a small rise, and it was so dark he couldn't see six feet in front of him. The wind picked up velocity and touched his face as he sat on the ground. Now he felt alone, free to think, and whatever he did, no one would laugh at him.

What am I doing here? he wondered. It seemed alien to his nature, to be alone in the middle of Texas, with a crew of cowboys and vaqueros, and a herd of longhorns. *How did I get here?*

He remembered the fight with Ephraim, ripping each other with their blades, and it seemed grotesque. How could he do such a thing? He touched his face, covered with bruises and cuts. He also was aware of pain all over his body, but somehow it was outside him, and at his center was peace and contentment.

He looked up at the endless black void, and tiny rays of light emanated from his fingertips. Far off in the distance, he heard the rumble of thunder. It was going to rain, but he didn't care. All he wanted to do was sit on the hill and feel the power of the cosmos surge through him.

It was as though he were floating in the air, looking down at himself. He realized how inconsequential he was, when compared with the infinitude of the universe. He, the other cowboys, and the herd would live and die, be forgotten, disappear into the sands of time, and no one would ever know or care about their effort to reach Abilene. They were poor lost clowns and fools, traveling across an endless range, for the amusement of God.

He heard footsteps, and thought the Comanches had returned. He rose to his feet and pulled his gun out of its holster as colored lights danced before his eyes. "Who's there!"

"Me," replied Cassandra. "Where are you, Johnny?"

"Up here."

He heard her approach, and then she came into view halfway up the rise. Her cowboy shirt was half-unbuttoned, she'd left her hat behind, and her hair was a profusion of gold. "What're you doing here?" she asked.

"Thinking."

"I don't feel well, Johnny. At first that stuff put me to sleep, but now I feel as if I'm . . . I don't know . . . as if I'm not real."

He gazed at the opening between her breasts, and a musky fragrance arose from her body. For a moment she looked like Marie, but fear was in her eyes. "What's in that stuff, Johnny?" she asked in a strange singsong voice. "What's it doing to us?"

Stone looked into the blackness, and on the horizon a faint squiggle of light appeared. "It's the medicine of the Great Spirit."

"I feel like I'm melting into the ground." She sat, and covered her face with her hands. "I'm so unhappy, Johnny. Nothing ever goes right for me."

He placed his arm around her shoulders. "It never goes right for anybody else either."

"When I was growing up, everything was easy, but now everything's so difficult."

Her face was inches away, he could feel her strong supple body, and remembered when she'd bathed naked in that stream a hundred thousand eons ago. Meanwhile, his closeness was making her nervous, and she pulled away. She looked at him, and he was a big blond male animal with a captivating smile, always so easy to be with. She knew that beneath his dirty bearded exterior, he'd be a gentleman.

She looked at the sky. "Might rain."

"Might," he agreed, his eyes roving over her body. The skin on her throat was smooth as satin; her breasts surged against her shirt, and her legs were long, nicely curved, and punctuated by cowboy boots. He felt a mad urge to reach over and unbutton her shirt, so he could see the treasures it concealed.

A man had to be honorable, no matter what Comanche medicine he'd eaten. He saw himself lying naked with her on the ground, and broke out in a cold sweat.

Cassandra thought she should run away, because she was having strange feelings. Rockets burst in the sky behind Stone's head, and she couldn't get up even if she wanted to. A deep, desperate emptiness gnawed inside her. The only man she'd ever slept with was her husband, thirty years older than she, and many times she'd wondered what a younger man might be like.

"I'm afraid," she said. "Maybe we should pray together."

They got to their knees, bowed their heads, and held hands.

"Dear God," she whispered, "please protect us, before we do something we shouldn't."

"Maybe I'd better go," he told her.

They were only inches apart in the night. Stone wanted to feel her naked skin, so everything would be all right. They looked at each other, as the night wind blew against them, rustling their hair. He saw a scrumptious young woman with the soul of an angel, and she saw a powerful man who could carry her to the farthest heights of her illicit hopes and dreams. They made jerky frightened movements toward each other, hesitated, and then she let out a cry like a wounded bird as he leaned forward and wrapped his arms around her. They squeezed each other with all their strength, and searched for each other's mouths.

He dug his fingernails into her back, and felt her breasts against his shirt. They kissed frantically, as if someone would tear them apart at any moment, and they couldn't stop now, even if someone held guns to their heads. He dug his hands into her hair and pressed his mouth against hers, and they bruised each other's lips, tasting each other's blood as they dropped to their knees on the ground.

She wanted to tell him to stop, but was swept away by hot kisses, and he held her as though he owned her. Snarling like a she-cat in heat, she clawed at his clothes, and she tore her shirt off her back as if it were paper. They were on their knees, bare-chested in front of each other, and he stared at those magnificent orbs that jiggled and wiggled ever so slightly in the breeze. She reached out her hands to him, and her head was cocked to one side, a tear rolling down her cheek. He fell into her arms, feeling her naked breasts against him, and they dropped to the ground, writhing against each other. She wrapped her legs around him, and he hugged her tightly as their mouths ground against each other, and their tongues wrestled.

Both knew they'd passed far over the edge, and could never return. Gone were the conventions of the world as their fingers sought each other's belts. They panted like dogs as they undressed each other, and no longer was it Cassandra the prim widow from New Orleans, and John Stone, ex-cavalry soldier, but primordial man and woman on the naked earth, with God above and hell below.

She moaned deep in her throat, and he growled like a beast as he pulled her remaining garments away. Finally they were naked, and stared at each other for a few moments, drinking in each other's bodies with their eyes, but they wanted more. Reaching forward, they clasped each other tightly, and then drank more deep droughts of ambrosia from their open thirsty mouths.

Stone thought nothing mattered except the delicious creature beneath him, who dug her fingers into his thick hair, as he buried his face between her breasts. It's what he'd wanted to do from the first moment he'd set eyes on her.

A cry escaped her lips as they rolled over the ground, clutching desperately, working their bodies without restraint, torn loose from the final gossamer strands of civilized behavior. Cassandra hoped it would last forever as Stone held her in his arms, his brain inflamed by mad lust. He couldn't take his mouth off her, as if she were the body and blood of life itself, far more satisfying than anything he'd ever tasted, a food that made him stronger than ever, and he knew what it was like to be a giant, or even a god.

Cassandra thought she was going to die as sweet flames engulfed her, while Stone sounded like the raging bull of the pampas. He felt as if lightning were shooting through him, transforming him into a luminous being that arced across the sky like a shooting star.

Light burst our of the heavens, and they heard a roll of thunder. They struggled against each other on the ground, pouring out all the love and passion of their souls, as huge drops of rain fell on their bodies.

And then, out of the depths of their most profound delirium madness, came the voice of Duke Truscott, ramrod of the Triangle Spur: *"Stampede!"*

12

EVERYONE RAN TOWARD the remuda as the heavens pealed with thunder and rain poured upon them. Huge spears of lightning rent the sky, forked, and shot into the ground. In the distance they could hear the hoofbeats of the herd.

"Stay with 'em, boys!" Truscott shouted, leaping onto his horse.

"Vamanos, muchachos!" yelled Don Emilio.

Stone climbed onto Tomahawk's back and turned him toward the cattle. The night was pitch-black, but then a bolt of lightning on the horizon illuminated the prairie, and the cowboys could see, for a brief second, longhorns in the distance, running for their lives.

Cassandra sped past Stone, whipping the haunches of her palomino, the wind creasing the brim of her cowboy hat. She knew the herd was decimated to half its strength, and if she lost this bunch, it'd mean the Last Chance Saloon. "Don't let 'em get away!" she hollered.

The cowboys and vaqueros galloped through the raging storm, and a bolt of light slammed into the ground, exploding a ton of dirt into the air. Cassandra and the men rode through the falling sod, and it pelted their hats and shirts as their horses streaked toward the cattle.

Something smacked Stone in the middle of his forehead, and he almost fell from Tomahawk's back. Hailstones large as hen's eggs fell around him, and a bolt of lightning struck a lone dead prairie tree, wreathing its scraggly top branches in dancing blue lights.

It was like an artillery bombardment in war, lightning bolts striking huge boulders and splitting them in two, while the most terrific explosive sounds tore through the atmosphere. The medicine of the Great Spirit still in him, John Stone thought he was back at Brandy Station, and Yankee shells rained upon him. His cavalry saber was in his hand and his yellow sash flew in the breeze behind him as he advanced toward the front rank of Yankees. Clouds of smoke drifted across the battlefield, and he couldn't see anything for a few harrowing moments, but then the smoke cleared and Stone gazed at blue uniforms directly ahead. The collision of two massive cavalry armies would occur in about a second, and for a moment Stone thought no one could survive the crush, but he grit his teeth and swung his old cavalry saber.

An incredible explosion shook the prairie, and a thick bolt of lightning wrote its unknowable word across the sky. Slipchuck could see the herd straight ahead, not more than a hundred yards away; they were gaining on it. The prairie was plunged into darkness again as Slipchuck slapped his reins against his horse's rump.

Gone was the gray from Slipchuck's mustache, and the bald spot on his head. He was twenty years old, this was his first stampede, and he was lean as a whiplash, with muscles like spring steel. Kid Slipchuck zoomed over the prairie, without the aches in his bones, the shortness of breath, and the lassitude that sometimes overtook him.

He was filled with the fire of youth, and carousels of bright colored lights flashed around him. "That injun dogshit's better'n any likker I ever had!" The hind legs of the drag appeared out of the blackness, and he realized he'd caught the herd. He pulled reins to the side, so he could come up on the right flank of the longhorns, and try to turn them.

Cassandra already had caught the right of the herd, and was zipping along, riding her palomino smoothly, bent low to present minimal resistance to the wind, but was only vaguely aware of what she was doing, felt no contact with the ground, and at times wasn't aware a horse was beneath her. She felt nothing could harm her, and when she became aware of the herd thundering a few feet to her left, she didn't care what happened to it, because the universe would go on, so would she, life was eternal, and so was the herd.

Don Emilio looked at her as he galloped past, and she was secure on her saddle as the most experienced vaquero; he wouldn't have to worry about her. He rode his favorite horse, Hermano, a lineback roan gelding with tremendous power and endurance, and urged him to his greatest effort, as he tried to reach the lead rank of longhorns.

Lightning was everywhere, ripping apart the night. Don Emilio saw it darting between the longhorn's legs and bouncing off their horns. There was forked lightning, chain lightning, and balls of lightning rolling across the ground, while the atmosphere thundered like the cannons of hell.

The cattle rushed through the night, terrorized by the terrible sights and sounds, while the cowboys' horses were maddened and running nearly wild. Don Emilio fought to keep his horse headed in a straight line toward the front of the herd, where he hoped to turn Old Ben. If he milled the herd, Cassandra would appreciate him more, and that's what he wanted, along with her smooth firm woman flesh in the moonlit stream. Everything he'd ever done in his life he'd done for women, so they'd love him, and this would be his finest hour. *I must have her, and this is the only way.*

He exulted in his manhood, and believed gringos were weaklings compared to caballeros such as himself. He was far ahead of all the other cowboys, and then heard hoofbeats to his right. He turned and saw the ramrod crouched low in his saddle, moving toward the front of the herd. Don Emilio urged his roan forward, but the ramrod pulled ahead easily, the front of his hat brim pressed back by the howling wind.

Truscott was making the ride of his life as the hooves of his fear-maddened horse ate the ground beneath them. The hailstorm had become blinding sheets of rain, the prairie slick as pig manure, but Truscott pressed onward, because nature had thrown down the gauntlet, and Truscott picked it up.

He too felt he must turn the herd, but not for Cassandra or any other earthly award. He wanted to prove to himself that he was the greatest ramrod in the world, and he could stop, single-handedly, the worst stampede he'd ever seen.

All his life he'd lived with longhorns, studied them, and knew what was going on in their minds. He was Duke Truscott, ramrod of the Triangle Spur, and no bunch of dumb cattle would dare defy his glory on this night of nights.

He turned the corner of the herd and moved toward the center, his lariat in his right hand, the reins gripped tightly in his left. The air smelled sulfurous, and a faint golden glow had come over the prairie. He looked at the cattle, and electricity played along their horns. A ball of fire the size of a plum rolled along a young steer's back.

And then Truscott's eyes fell on Old Ben, and Truscott knew if he could turn him, he could turn the herd. He grabbed a handful of reins and pulled his horse's head toward Old Ben, but the horse was terrified and didn't want to go. The horse struggled to escape, but the bit dug into his gums and made them bleed. Reluctantly the horse turned toward the charging cattle.

"Ho there!" Truscott hollered in his deepest ramrod voice, and afterward, every cowboy in the crew would say they'd heard him, no matter where they'd been. "Ho cow! Move out my goddamn road!"

Truscott's horse galloped toward Old Ben, and Truscott leaned forward, staring into Old Ben's terrified eyes. It was a test of will, his against the dumb brute's, and Truscott had to prevail.

The herd trampled closer, and Truscott's horse could see imminent destruction worse even than the bit in his mouth. He turned away, and Truscott stood in his stirrups, pulling the reins with every sinew in his body, twisting the horse's head.

The horse lost his balance, and crashed onto his back. Truscott's leg was trapped beneath the horse, a solid bolt of pain shot through him, and he raised his gnarled hand before Old Ben's drooling snout.

"Turn, damn you—you son of a whore! Ho there!"

Old Ben saw only the horrifying lightning storm. He and hundreds of other longhorns rampaged toward Truscott, and Truscott realized he wasn't going to turn them. He shook his fist at the fear-crazed longhorns and bared his teeth, raging furiously as he fell beneath their terrible bludgeoning hooves.

Lightning crackled across the sky, and the herd was bathed in a weird phosphorescent glow as thunder reverberated off distant mountains. Brandy Station had vanished, Stone was in Texas, Cassandra's herd was running wild, and the only thing to do was get in front with the other cowboys and try to mill them. Spurring Tomahawk, he flew through gold crystals as the herd spread out beside him like a living rolling blanket.

Stone felt strong, confident, and he'd just made love to a beautiful woman. Now the difficult seemed easy, and the impossible only a minor challenge for a man as incredible as Stone felt at that moment. He steered Tomahawk toward the herd, and Tomahawk didn't want to go, because he was badly spooked by the bizarre events of the night, and the prairie was yellow and blue, with little spheres of fire dancing upon it.

"C'mon!" Stone yelled, pulling Tomahawk closer to the longhorns, and Tomahawk was so unsure of himself, he gave up resistance. His boss seemed to know what he was doing—let him call the shots.

Stone sat light on his saddle, and Tomahawk felt as if Stone were an appendage of his body. He knew what Stone wanted, and was sure Stone would die, but if that was Stone's intention, Tomahawk would die with him.

Tomahawk angled closer to the herd, and now that it was close, Stone could see the individual longhorns only a few feet apart, and in some places actually touched and rubbed against each other. Tiny marbles of fire rolled from horn to horn, and blast furnace heat emanated from their bodies. Stone felt it sear his eyes and cheeks, and now he was close enough to jump from his saddle onto their backs.

Something told him it was a foolhardy thing to do, and Tomahawk whinnied his disapproval, but someday, at a campfire, Stone would tell his grandson about the night he'd walked across a herd of stampeding cattle. He raised himself in his saddle, drew one leg over the pommel, and leapt into the air. He experienced a sinking sensation, and then one boot came down on a steer's back. Stone caught his balance, bobbled, and jumped onto another steer. When he landed he leaned to the left, leaned to the right, and then stabilized himself, bending his knees to absorb the jostling of the animal as it clobbered the plains.

I've done it! Stone thought. But the steer beneath him was frightened even more by the presence of Stone on his back, and raised his front hooves into the air, just as Stone was jumping toward the back of the next longhorn.

Stone lost his balance, and this time couldn't catch it. A terrible desperate feeling came over him as he slipped down the side of the cow's wet back. Hooves tore up the grass before his eyes, and he knew he'd always been too impulsive, with far too high an opinion of his abilities, and he saw the Gypsy laughing behind a mound of earth.

He plummeted toward the ground, and a long black arm extended out of the sky, grabbing hold of his bicep. Stone bounced on the turf, and then was pulled upward. He turned around and saw Ephraim atop his horse, bareheaded, dragging him away from the stampeding cattle. Stone dived for Ephraim's waist, held on, kicked the ground, and vaulted into the saddle behind Ephraim, who pulled his horse's reins to the right, to get away from the herd.

Stone had been six inches from a gruesome death, but they still weren't home free. Cattle swirled around them like eddies in a fast-moving river, but miraculously none of them ran into the horse and two riders, another eerie experience the longhorns wanted to avoid. Ephraim's horse reached the edge of the stampede and broke away from the cattle. In the distance, Stone could see Tomahawk galloping wildly, stirrups flapping in the air, trying to escape the lightning.

When they were a healthy distance from the herd, Ephraim pulled back his reins. The horse came to a stop, and Ephraim climbed down from the saddle. He dropped prostrate on the ground, his chest heaving.

"You damned fool," he uttered.

Stone jumped to the grass and sat heavily, hearing the herd stampede into the farthest reaches of the night. His hand shook as he pulled his bag of tobacco out of his shirt pocket, and he knew Ephraim was right, he'd tried something more stupid than ever, even worse than blundering onto the bear, and nearly killed himself. A dangerous heedless folly was deep inside him, and he had to get to the bottom of it before it was too late. But then a new thought pressed into his mind. He lit the cigarette, tossed the bag of tobacco to Ephraim, and asked, "Why'd you do it?"

Ephraim looked at him. "I told you before, white boy. If anybody's a-gonna kill you, it's a-gonna be *me*."

Stone thought that over for a few moments as Ephraim rolled a cigarette. Then Stone looked coldly at Ephraim and said, "A man doesn't risk his life to save his worst enemy. Tell me the truth for a change."

Ephraim lit his cigarette, and gazed off into the distance as the rain pelted them, washing away dirt and dried blood. "I told you," he said. "So's I can kill you myself."

"If you despise me as much as you say, it doesn't fit together, unless you're crazy. Is that what it is, Ephraim? Are you crazy?"

Ephraim threw the tobacco toward Stone, then turned away. "I don't want to look at you. I hate your guts, and I live for the day I can piss on yer grave."

"You could have been pissing on it tomorrow morning, if that's what you'd wanted." Stone moved in front of Ephraim and grabbed his shoulder roughly as he screamed: "Why'd you save my life?"

Ephraim pulled his shoulder out of Stone's grasp and turned in another direction, but Stone moved so Ephraim would be forced to look at him. Ephraim raised himself to his feet and balled his fists. "Git away from me, white boy,'cause I'll kill you!"

Stone stood opposite Ephraim and squared his shoulders as a bolt of lightning shot across the sky. Stone's hat had blown off, and the wind and rain blew against his face as he screamed: "You're a liar! You're hiding something!"

"Git out my face, white boy! I had just about enough of your shit!"

"You don't have the guts to tell the truth! You're a coward!"

Ephraim furled his thick lips. "Don't you call me no coward, if you wants to go on livin', you white son of a bitch!"

"What else can I call a man who's afraid to say the truth? To hell with you, if you haven't got the guts to speak your mind! You're just another dumb nigra, far as I'm concerned, or maybe you really like me in some strange way, though you don't have the guts to admit it!"

Stone turned angrily and walked away. Tomahawk was out there someplace, and he was going to kick his ass for letting him attempt the stunt with the cattle. Stone walked several steps, then heard Ephraim behind him. He spun around and pulled out his knife, because he expected one in the back.

Ephraim's hands were empty, and his jaw trembled as he spoke. "I'll tell you, becuzz I ain't no coward, and I don't want you thinkin' I *like* you, or I saved you for anything *you* ever did. You want to know why? You think you can handle it, white boy?"

"This white boy can handle anything you've got, nigra."

Ephraim paused and looked away from Stone. He was silent for a few moments as he collected his thoughts, and then he said, "There was a time befo' the war when your daddy was havin' money trubble. Don't reckon you even knowed about it,'cause you was away at West Point at the time, but anyways, your daddy planned to sell some of us, and a man made him a cash offer for me and my brother."

Ephraim paused again, and shivered as if at the North Pole; Stone could see this wasn't easy for him. "Well," Ephraim continued, "that night my momma went to your daddy, and got down on her knees, and begged him not to break up the family. She even kissed his feet, and you could hear her wailin' all over the damn place, and your daddy finally said he wouldn't break up her family no matter what happened, and he'd set us free 'fo' he'd sell us separate."

Ephraim turned toward Stone and looked him unflinchingly in the eye. "So you wants to know why I saved your ass? It was fo' your daddy, fo' the one good thing he ever did in his life! That's why! Now you know!" Ephraim reached to his belt and pulled out his butcher knife. "I guess there's only one mo' thing we got to do now!"

Stone held his Apache knife in his hand. "You said my daddy went to the slave quarters at night, with the slave women. Was that true, or was it a lie?"

"It was the truth, and I'll tell you somethin' else, one of the women he came to see was *my mother*!"

Stone lowered his knife, pushed it into the scabbard in his boot, and no longer had the stomach to fight this man.

Ephraim continued: "Do you remember your daddy used to 'spirement with chickens? Well, I used to take care of 'em, and one of the things they did was crossbreed 'em to see what they'd get. I remember one time a black hen and a white rooster got together. I saw the black hen lay her three eggs, and I waited till they hatched, and she had two white chicks, and one black chick, even though his father was *completely white*.

I used to think about that a lot, and I ain't never forgot it. Do you understand what I'm sayin', Massa John? I mean, do you *really* understand what I'm sayin'?"

"You're saying we might be brothers."

Ephraim moaned, and all the strength went out of him. He sank to the ground and buried his face in his hands. "I hate you," he said, "and I hated you all my life."

Stone dropped to one knee in front of him. "Ephraim, I never bought or sold a slave in my life, I never whipped one, and I never forced myself into any mother's bed. Maybe my daddy did some of those things, but God will judge him, not you. My daddy came from a world where that happened all the time, and he didn't know any better, but who knows, if things were different, maybe we might've been the slaves, and you the slave owners. Your own people in Africa sold you to the Yankee ship captains, so don't preach to me. You don't really think nigras're any better in their hearts than white people, do you?"

"You're damn right I do!" Ephraim shouted.

The two sat silently for a long time, as the rain baptized them, and lightning bolts cracked the sky.

13

IT WAS MORNING, the sky still was cloudy, and the dead lay on the ground next to a big hole scooped out of the muddy earth. Not far away sprawled the herd, not more than one thousand head of cattle now, and the rest were littered across North Texas. The first job was round them up, although the crew had no chuck wagon, no tools, and nothing but their guns, horses, and plenty of beef to eat.

But first they had to bury their dead. The survivors stood around the hole and looked at Duke Truscott, ramrod of the Triangle Spur. They could make out his general form, and some of his clothing, but everything was matted with blood. Don Emilio had seen him go down, and told the others Truscott tried to stop Old Ben single-handedly, but the herd hadn't stopped, and now he was mangled beyond recognition.

It was time for Cassandra to say her final prayer, but somehow no words came to her mouth. For a man like Truscott, there was nothing anyone could say. She realized now she'd loved the leathery old bastard. He'd been her father, big brother, and sometimes she'd thought about being alone with him, for she always had a weakness for older men.

Now he was dead, and her eyes were salty with tears. She knew Duke Truscott didn't approve of tears, but she couldn't hold them back. Her body was wracked by a sob, and every cowboy and vaquero wept silently alongside her, because he was their fallen leader, and everyone admired him. When they came right down to it, they knew Duke Truscott had been utterly fearless, and that's what every man, deep down, wishes he had more than anything else.

They all knew they'd never forget him. He'd been stubborn and too harsh sometimes, but never asked them to do anything he wouldn't. He shared their pain and pleasure, and was the kind of man other men followed, because he was solid as a rock. The only thing that could stop Truscott was a herd of stampeding cattle, so that's what he went up against, to see what it was like.

He'd found out you can't push too far, and everybody standing at the grave learned the lesson from him. The school of the open range was unforgiving, and Truscott had been their professor, with his life as his blackboard.

Cassandra realized Truscott had made her stronger, because he'd fought her tooth and nail, and if she could stand up to Duke Truscott, she'd never be afraid of anybody again in her life. There were times he'd given in to her when he didn't have to, she knew now, although he could've put her over his knee and spanked her whenever he felt like it, and she couldn't've stopped him. Evidently in his own rough way he'd cared about her, and he never let her down.

She remembered the time he'd come to her and said she had more balls than most men he'd known. That meant, in his tough cowboy language, that she had guts, and coming from a man like Truscott, who wasn't afraid of anything, that was high praise indeed.

She wanted to end the drive, because too many men had died. She even wished she could fall on the ground and weep her eyes out, but she knew Truscott, wherever he was now, wouldn't stand for it. He'd tear the floorboards out of hell, because it was his herd too, and a point of honor to push it all the way to Abilene. Now she had two reasons to move those longhorns up the trail—for herself, but also for old Duke Truscott, the greatest ramrod who ever lived.

And she knew what he'd say just then if he were standing there with them, in his old rawhide vest and his floppy leggins, with his Remington hanging low on his waist. She put on her hat, and slanted the brim over her eyes the way he always did. "We got work to do!" she hollered, hitching her thumbs in her gunbelt, her eyes brimming with tears. "Fill that goddamned hole—and let's move it out!"

NELSON NYE
The Baron of Blood & Thunder

Two-time winner of the Western Writers of America's Golden Spur Award, and winner of the Levi Strauss Golden Saddleman Award... with over 50,000,000 copies of his books in print.

NELSON NYE

Author of *RIDER ON THE ROAN, TROUBLE AT QUINN'S CROSSING, THE SEVEN SIX-GUNNERS, THE PARSON OF GUNBARREL BASIN, LONG RUN, GRINGO, THE LOST PADRE, TREASURE TRAIL FROM TUCSON,* and dozens of others is back with his most exciting Western adventure yet..

THE LAST CHANCE KID

Born to English nobility, Alfred Addlington wants nothing more than to become an American cowboy. With his family's reluctant permission, Alfred becomes just that... and gets much more than he bargained for when he gets mixed up with horse thieves, crooked ranchers, and a band of prairie rats who implicate him in one crime after another!

Turn the page
for an exciting preview of
THE LAST CHANCE KID
by Nelson Nye!

On sale now,
wherever Jove Books are sold!

MY NAME IS Alfred Addlington. Some may find it hard to believe I was born in New York City. I never knew my mother. Father is a lord; I suppose you would him a belted earl. The family never cared for Mother. Marrying a commoner if you are of the nobility is far worse, it was felt, than murdering someone.

I was, of course, educated in England. As a child I'd been an avid reader, and always at the back of my mind was this horrible obsession to one day become a Wild West cowboy. I'd no need to run away—transportation was happily furnished. While I was in my seventeenth year my youthful peccadillos were such that I was put on a boat bound for America, made an allowance and told never to come back.

They've been hammering outside. I have been in this place now more than four months and would never have believed it could happen to me, but the bars on my window are truly there, and beyond the window they are building a gallows. So I'd better make haste if I'm to get this all down.

I do not lay my being here to a "broken home" or evil companions. I like to feel in some part it is only a matter of justice miscarried, though I suppose most any rogue faced with the rope is bound to consider himself badly used. But you shall judge for yourself.

Seventeen I was when put aboard that boat, and I had a wealth of experience before at nineteen this bad thing caught up with me.

So here I was again in America. In a number of ways it was a peculiar homecoming. First thing I did after clearing customs was get aboard a train that would take me into those great open spaces I'd so long been entranced with. It brought me to New Mexico and a town called Albuquerque, really an overgrown village from which I could see the Watermellon Mountains.

I found the land and the sky and the brilliant sunshine remarkably stimulating. Unlike in the British Midlands the air was clean and crisply invigorating. But no one would have me. At the third ranch I tried they said, "Too young. We got no time to break in a raw kid with roundup scarce two weeks away."

At that time I'd no idea of the many intricacies or the harsh realities of the cow business. You might say I had on a pair of rose-colored glasses. I gathered there might be quite a ruckus building up in Lincoln County, a sort of large-scale feud from all I could learn, so I bought myself a horse, a pistol and a J. B. Stetson hat and headed for the action.

In the interests of saving time and space I'll only touch on the highlights of these preliminaries, recording full details where events became of impelling importance.

Passing through Seven Oaks, I met Billy, a chap whose name was on everyone's tongue, though I could not think him worth half the talk. To me he seemed hard, mean spirited and stupid besides. He made fun of my horse, calling it a crowbait, declared no real gent would be found dead even near it. Turned out he knew of a first class mount he'd be glad to secure for me if I'd put one hundred dollars into his grubby hand. He was a swaggering sort I was glad to be rid of. Feeling that when in Rome one did as the Romans, I gave him the hundred dollars, not expecting ever to see him again, but hoping in these strange surroundings I would not be taken for a gullible "greenhorn."

A few days later another chap, who said his name was Jesse Evans, advised me to steer clear of Billy. "A bad lot," he told me. "A conniving double-crosser." When I mentioned giving Billy the hundred dollars on the understanding he would provide a top horse, he said with a snort and kind of pitying look, "You better bid that money good-bye right now."

But three days later, true to his word, Billy rode up to the place I was lodging with a fine horse in tow. During my schooling back in England I had learned quite a bit about horses, mostly hunters and hacks and jumpers and a few that ran in "flat" races for purses, and this mount Billy fetched looked as good as the best. "Here, get on him," Billy urged. "See what you think, and if he won't do I'll find you another."

"He'll do just fine," I said, taking the lead shank, "and here's ten dollars for your kindness."

With that lopsided grin he took the ten and rode off.

I rode the new horse over to the livery and dressed him in my saddle and bridle while the proprietor eyed me with open mouth. "Don't tell me that's yours," he finally managed, still looking as if he couldn't believe what he saw.

"He surely is. Yes, indeed. Gave a hundred dollars for him."

Just as I was about to mount up, a mustached man came bustling into the place. "Stop right there!" this one said across the glint of a pistol. "I want to know what you're doing with the Major's horse. Speak up or it'll be the worse for you."

"What Major?"

"Major Murphy. A big man around here."

"Never heard of him. I bought this horse for one hundred dollars."

"Bought it, eh? Got a bill of sale?"

"Well, no," I said. "Didn't think to ask for one."

I'd discovered by this time the man with the gun had a star on his vest. His expression was on the skeptical side. He wheeled on the liveryman. "You sell him that horse?"

"Not me! Came walkin' in here with it not ten minutes ago."

"I'm goin' to have to hold you, young feller," the man with the star said, pistol still aimed at my belt buckle. "A horse thief's the lowest scoundrel I know of."

A shadow darkened the doorway just then and Jesse Evans stepped in. "Hang on a bit, Marshal. I'll vouch for this button. If he told you he paid for this horse it's the truth. Paid it to Billy—I'll take my oath on it."

A rather curious change reshaped the marshal's features. "You sure of that, Evans?"

"Wouldn't say so if I wasn't."

The marshal looked considerably put out. "All right," he said to me, "looks like you're cleared. But I'm confiscatin' this here horse; I'll see it gits back to the rightful owner. You're free to go, but don't let me find you round here come sundown." And he went off with the horse.

"Never mind," Evans said. "Just charge it up to experience. But was I you I'd take the marshal's advice and hunt me another habitation." And he grinned at me sadly. "I mean pronto—right now."

Still rummaging my face, he said, scrubbing a fist across his own, "Tell you what I'll do," and led me away out of the livery-keeper's hearing. "I've got a reasonably good horse I'll let you have for fifty bucks. Even throw in a saddle—not so handsome as the one you had but durable and sturdy. You interested?"

Once stung, twice shy. "Let's see him," I said, and followed him out to a corral at the far edge of town. I looked the horse over for hidden defects but could find nothing wrong with it; certainly the animal should be worth fifty dollars. Firmly I said, "I'll be wanting a bill of sale."

"Of course," he chuckled. "Naturally." Fetching a little blue notebook out of a pocket, he asked politely, "What name do you go by?"

"My own," I said. "Alfred Addlington."

He wrote it down with a flourish. "All right, Alfie." He tore the page from his book and I put it in my wallet while Jesse saddled and bridled my new possession. I handed him the money, accepted the reins and stepped into the saddle.

He said, "I'll give you a piece of advice you can take or cock a snook at. Notice you're packin' a pistol. Never put a hand anyplace near it without you're aimin' to use it. Better still," he said, looking me over more sharply, "get yourself a shotgun, one with two barrels. Nobody'll laugh at that kind of authority."

"Well, thanks. Where do I purchase one?"

"Be a-plenty at Lincoln if that's where you're headed. Any gun shop'll have 'em."

I thanked him again and, having gotten precise directions, struck out for the county seat feeling I'd been lucky to run across such a good Samaritan. I was a pretty fair shot with handgun or rifle but had discovered after much practice I could be killed and buried before getting my pistol into speaking position. So Evans's advice about acquiring a shotgun seemed additional evidence of the good will he bore me.

It was shortly after noon the next day when I came up the dirt road into Lincoln. For all practical purposes it was a one-street town, perhaps half a mile long, flanked by business establishments, chief amongst them being the two-storey Murphy-Dolan store building. I recall wondering if this was the Major whose stolen horse Billy'd sold me, later discovering it was indeed. Leaving my horse at a hitch rack I went inside to make inquiries about finding a job.

The gentleman I talked with had an Irish face underneath a gray derby. After listening politely he informed me he was Jimmie Dolan—the Dolan of the establishment, and could offer me work as a sort of handyman if such wasn't beneath my dignity. If I showed aptitude, he said, there'd be a better job later and he would start me off at fifty cents a day.

I told him I'd take it.

"If you've a horse there's a carriage shed back of the store where you can leave him and we'll sell you oats at a discount," he added.

"I'd been hoping to get on with some ranch," I said.

"A fool's job," said Dolan with a grimace. "Long hours, hard work, poor pay and no future," he assured me. "You string your bets with us and you'll get to be somebody while them yahoos on ranches are still punchin' cows."

I went out to feed, water and put up my new horse. There was a man outside giving it some pretty hard looks. "This your nag?" he asked as I came up.

"It most certainly is."

"Where'd you get it?"

"Bought it in Seven Oaks a couple of days ago. Why?"

He eyed me some more. "Let's see your bill of sale, bub," and brushed back his coat to display a sheriff's badge pinned to his shirt.

I dug out the paper I had got from Evans. The sheriff studied it and then, much more searching, studied me. "Expect you must be new around here if you'd take Evans's word for anything. I'm taking it for granted you bought the horse in good faith, but I'm going to have to relieve you of it. This animal's the property of a man named Tunstall, stolen from him along with several others about a week ago."

I was pretty riled up. "This," I said angrily, "is the second stolen mount I've been relieved of in the past ten days. Don't you have any honest men in your bailiwick?"

"A few, son. Not many I'll grant you. You're talkin' to one now as it happens."

"Then where can I come by a horse that's not stolen?"

That blue stare rummaged my face again. "You a limey?"

"If you mean do I hail from England, yes. I came here hoping to get to be a cowboy but nobody'll have me."

He nodded. "It's a hard life, son, an' considerably underpaid. Takes time to learn, but you seem young enough to have plenty of that. How much did you give for the two stolen horses?"

"One hundred and fifty dollars."

He considered me again. "You're pretty green, I guess. Most horses in these parts sell for forty dollars."

"A regular Johnny Raw," I said bitterly.

"Well . . . a mite gullible," the sheriff admitted. "Reckon time will cure that if you live long enough. Being caught with a stolen horse hereabouts is a hangin' offense. Come along," he said. "I'll get you a horse there's no question about, along with a bona fide set of papers to prove it. Do you have forty dollars?"

I told him I had and, counting out the required sum, handed it to him. He picked up the reins of Tunstall's horse, and we walked down the road to a public livery and feed corral. The sheriff told the man there what we wanted and the fellow fetched out a good-looking sorrel mare.

"This here's a mite better'n average, Sheriff—oughta fetch eighty. Trouble is these fool cowhands won't ride anythin' but geldin's. I guarantee this mare's a real goer. Try her out, boy. If you ain't satisfied, she's yours fer forty bucks."

The sheriff, meanwhile, had got my gear off Tunstall's horse. "Get me a lead shank," he said to the stableman. Transferring my saddle and bridle to the mare I swung onto her, did a few figure eights, put her into a lope, walked her around and proclaimed myself satisfied. The animal's name it seemed was Singlefoot. "She'll go all day at that rockin' chair gate," the man said. "Comfortable as two six-shooters in the same belt."

Thanking them both, I rode her over to the nearest café, tied her securely to the hitch pole in front of it and went in to put some food under my belt, pleased to see she looked very well alongside the tail-switchers already tied there.

Classic Westerns from
GILES TIPPETTE

Justa Williams is a bold young Texan who doesn't usually set out looking for trouble...but somehow he always seems to find it.

__BAD NEWS 0-515-10104-4/$3.95

Justa Williams finds himself trapped in Bandera, a tough town with an unusual notion of justice. Justa's accused of a brutal murder that he didn't commit. So his two fearsome brothers have to come in and bring their own brand of justice.

__CROSS FIRE 0-515-10391-8/$3.95

A herd of illegally transported Mexican cattle is headed toward the Half-Moon ranch—and with it, the likelihood of deadly Mexican tick fever. The whole county is endangered... and it looks like it's up to Justa to take action.

__JAILBREAK 0-515-10595-3/$3.95

Justa gets a telegram saying there's squatters camped on the Half-Moon ranch, near the Mexican border. Justa's brother, Norris, gets in a whole heap of trouble when he decides to investigate. But he winds up in a Monterrey jail for punching a Mexican police captain, and Justa's got to figure out a way to buy his brother's freedom.

For Visa, MasterCard and American Express orders ($10 minimum) call: 1-800-631-8571

FOR MAIL ORDERS: CHECK BOOK(S). FILL OUT COUPON. SEND TO:

BERKLEY PUBLISHING GROUP
390 Murray Hill Pkwy., Dept. B
East Rutherford, NJ 07073

NAME_____

ADDRESS_____

CITY_____

STATE_____ZIP_____

PLEASE ALLOW 6 WEEKS FOR DELIVERY.
PRICES ARE SUBJECT TO CHANGE WITHOUT NOTICE.

POSTAGE AND HANDLING:
$1.50 for one book, 50¢ for each additional. Do not exceed $4.50.

BOOK TOTAL $ _____

POSTAGE & HANDLING $ _____

APPLICABLE SALES TAX $ _____
(CA, NJ, NY, PA)

TOTAL AMOUNT DUE $ _____

PAYABLE IN US FUNDS.
(No cash orders accepted.)